LOVE BETWEEN THE LINES

LOVE
BETWEEN THE
LINES

•

CATHY FORSYTHE

AVALON BOOKS
THOMAS BOUREGY AND COMPANY, INC.
401 LAFAYETTE STREET
NEW YORK, NEW YORK 10003

PRINTED IN THE UNITED STATES OF AMERICA
ON ACID-FREE PAPER
BY HADDON CRAFTSMEN, SCRANTON, PENNSYLVANIA

To Marcia Markland, for continuing to make
my dreams come true.

Chapter One

"When I heard you were sitting at home, pouting, I didn't believe it. But I guess it's true."

Russ turned with a guilty start, glaring at the blond-haired woman silhouetted in the doorway. "I'm not pouting." He shifted, leaning heavily on his cane.

She glanced around the room, taking in the drawn shades, the depressing stillness. "Trust me, Russ Connor, you're pouting."

"Real men don't pout."

Victoria sighed, planting her fists on her jean-clad hips. "You shouldn't set yourself up like that, Connor. I could take your fragile male ego out with nothing more than a short

1

sentence. But I'm feeling nice today. I'll let you live your fantasy a little longer.''

She stretched to reach the cord of the window shade, tugging it to let the Colorado sunlight pour into the room. Russ squinted, not wanting to be tempted by her or the warm sunshine, and turned away.

''Kelly said you needed a swift kick, but I think she's wrong.'' Victoria paused, waiting for him to look up. ''I think it will take a baseball bat applied right between the eyes just to get your attention.''

Russ glared back, trying to ignore the intensity in her blue eyes. ''Kelly's my ex-partner, not my mother.''

''True. I guess because you did a little matchmaking for her and Jayk, she thinks she owes you. Go figure.''

''Go away, Victoria.'' He turned his back on her, knowing she wouldn't take the hint.

''No. We're going for a drive. And if you're nice, I'll let you buy me dinner.''

''I can't drive yet. Doctor's orders.'' He massaged his thigh, trying to rub away the dull ache that had become his constant companion, determined not to let her get to him like she usually did.

''Well, I *do* have a driver's license. Women have that right now, you know.''

He clenched his teeth, struggling to keep his anger under control. "I don't feel like going out."

She moved closer, her determination glaring from her eyes like sharp daggers. "You'll go out, one way or the other. We can do this the easy way, or the hard way—your choice."

"You sound like a bad cop movie, Vicky. Just go away. I'm not your problem." He felt a brief flare of satisfaction at using the nickname she hated, but it faded much too quickly.

"Don't call me Vicky." The words were an old chant, said in a tired tone of voice. "And you *are* my problem. At least for now. I owe you and I figure this is a fairly safe method of paying you back."

"You don't owe me. We've been through that before. I was doing my job, nothing more."

She stepped closer, tipping her head slightly to meet his dark glare. "I don't agree. But then we've never managed to agree on much, have we? I'm here to pay my debt of honor, so get with it and let me do my civic duty. Then I can get back to my work and you can return to your pouting."

His voice came out louder than he'd intended. "I'm not—"

She held up a hand to halt his words. "I

know, you're not pouting. It's a matter of perspective. Get a move on, Connor. I have a job to get back to. Not all of us have the luxury of sitting around all day—not pouting.''

''You're not big enough or mean enough to make me do anything. Just give it up.'' He sat down in his favorite chair, daring her to make him do her bidding.

''You know me better than that.''

Russ almost groaned as he struggled to tamp down his growing frustration. Unfortunately, he did know her. Once Victoria Stephens got something into her head, there was no way to deter her. He could stand and argue with her for the rest of the afternoon, but all he'd accomplish was making himself hoarse. He knew she'd spend the entire night making his life miserable if that was what it took to achieve whatever she'd set out to do.

She studied him and he could almost hear her thoughts churning. ''I had to learn how to use a lasso for a story last year. I could always resort to that, I guess.''

He wanted to protest, to put her in her place, but settled for a glare that had often made the most determined fighter back down.

''At least I finally have your attention.'' She pushed open the front door and smiled. ''Get your shoes on and let's go. It's time for you to return to the real world.''

Russ glanced down at his well-worn slippers, then watched Victoria step outside. He sighed and dragged a hand through his hair, the shaggy brown mane badly in need of a cut. She wouldn't leave him alone until he gave in, he was certain of that. And it was tempting to get outside, just for a little bit. Since he'd been shot, life had revolved around visits to the doctor, physical therapy, and an aching emptiness he couldn't seem to fill.

Bracing himself, he climbed out of the chair and worked his way to the bedroom, leaning heavily on the cane. He didn't really mind the pain, the never-ending throb. It reminded him he was still alive. At least physically.

And he wanted to live. He just wasn't sure he remembered how. The department had been his life and his love for too many years. Now that his career had been snatched away from him, he was drifting aimlessly, not having the energy or the strength to make a plan, to think things through.

A car horn blared outside and Russ allowed himself a small twist of his lips. She'd lean on that thing all afternoon if he didn't come out. The last thing he needed today was one of his buddies from the station coming by on a noise complaint.

As he passed the dresser, he glanced in the mirror and frowned. It was day three for this T-shirt and it was looking worse than bad. He grabbed a button-down shirt from the closet and slipped it on, feeling his mood lift a fraction above the usual despair.

The horn honked again.

Russ leaned over, struggling with his old tennis shoes as his leg protested the stretch. By the time he finished that little chore, sweat stood out on his forehead and his breath was a sharp rasp in his throat. This from a man who had once run three miles a day in addition to pumping weights and swimming laps.

He leaned his forehead on hands that were folded across the top of the cane.

Why bother? Why keep trying?

The horn blared.

Because Victoria would harass him even in death if he didn't get out to that car soon. The image of her trying to lasso his wandering spirit brought the closest thing to a smile his lips had seen in too many months.

He grabbed his sunglasses from the dresser and slipped them on. Another reminder of days in the past, days never to be relived. Sunglasses had been an important part of his equipment as a cop. The mirrored lenses tended to disconcert people and they said things they'd never intended. Maybe the tactic would work on Victoria. But probably not.

A double tap sounded on the horn this time.

She was getting mad. And even Russ knew better than to make Victoria too mad. She made Attila the Hun look tame when she was in a full rage.

He limped outside and slowly struggled down the three steps at the front of the small house. Victoria simply watched, no trace of sympathy in her eyes. Russ felt some relief, knowing he wouldn't be able to tolerate her pity. It was hard enough from his friends, but unacceptable from Victoria. He opened the door and forced his leg to bend enough so he could edge into the passenger seat. The relief when he was finally settled threatened to escape in a deep sigh but he held it back.

As soon as his door closed, she jammed the car into reverse and swung into the street. Russ gritted his teeth and groped for the armrest.

''I left the top down so you could get some sunshine. You look like a sick old man.''

''Thanks. I knew I could count on you to cheer me up.'' He grabbed for another hand-hold as she took the next corner a little faster than he'd have liked. Finally, he was able to let go long enough to dig out the seat belt and snap it on.

He closed his eyes as the wind blew through his hair. He couldn't help but savor the air, the warmth . . . the light. It felt fresh, clean, alive. Maybe he *had* been pouting. But he'd never admit Victoria had been right.

The silence settled between them, comfortable silence that didn't need to be filled. Russ finally opened his eyes and looked around, surprised to see that little had changed during his three months of confinement.

"Do you need to do anything, run errands or something?"

Her voice shattered the feelings creeping over him, feelings he wasn't yet ready to recognize. "So far, I've managed to have what I need delivered. But I'm certain I could find a few good *friends* to help me out."

"Forget it, Connor. This is a onetime deal. I won't be your nursemaid or your errand girl." She twirled the wheel, throwing Russ into the side of the car. "Come to think of it, there's a nice old lady down the hall from me who's looking for something to do. Maybe she'd take on the care and feeding of a grouchy young man."

"Don't worry, I'll make out by myself." The loneliness came back, taunting him with how his life had changed in less than a heart-beat of time.

"I know she'd be happy to—"

"Vicky."

Victoria clamped her lips together, but he could see the edges of her mouth trembling as she tried to hold back her laughter.

Silence drifted between them again.

"There's been another robbery." Her voice was quiet, but her words echoed through his thoughts, threatening the little scrap of peace he'd managed to gain.

"Where?" The word came out much more harshly than he'd intended. "Are there any leads?"

Victoria glanced at him before answering. "No, the cops don't have a thing. It was at Anderson's Jewelry. Yesterday. Only took the good stuff, as usual."

"Someone knows what they want."

She nodded, her lips pressed together. "So do I. I want the entire story, all to myself. I've already got two good leads."

"Turn it over to the police, Victoria."

"No. This is *my* investigation. I could get some real recognition for a story like this."

"You're a reporter, lady. Not a cop. Let the pros handle it."

"I *am* a pro, an investigative reporter, and

I'm investigating. If I just happen to break the case wide open for the police, it'll be a lucky break for them.''

His anger came, swift and deadly. ''They almost killed me. Don't you get it? I had a gun, a radio, backup, and I still got shot. You have nothing to protect you except a brain that's two sizes too small and constantly trying to get you into trouble.''

She took one hand from the wheel and rested it gently on his injured leg. His muscles jumped at her touch, but he forced himself to ignore the warmth she generated.

''I'm sorry, Russ. We've had our bad moments, but I'd never have wished this on you.'' The car finally broke free of the city limits and she accelerated. ''I have a job to do too. And I don't intend to quit trying to find out who's behind these robberies.''

He struggled, trying to tamp down the frustration, the anger. She was out there digging, nosing around, doing the job he so desperately wanted to do. It made him want to strike out, to hurt someone in return. But he didn't want Victoria to be the one who received the brunt of his frustration. The woman still held a tiny corner of his heart, just enough to make him interested. But he'd never tell her that.

Needing a change of subject, he glanced at

the speedometer. "You can get a ticket for driving this fast, you know."

"Yeah." She grinned and shook her shoulder-length hair out into the wind. "But this is my therapy. Sit back and enjoy it. If I get stopped, I know you'll fix things for me."

He tried to relax. He really tried. But he couldn't stop his brain from cataloging every movement around them, couldn't keep his eyes from recording license numbers and checking drivers' faces. Old habits died hard, but this one might never let go.

The despair crept back and Russ knew he was fighting a losing battle. Police work was his life. If he couldn't have that, there was nothing left. He closed his eyes against the anguish flooding through him. The doctor had said there was still a chance, but deep inside, Russ knew the odds were against him.

The car slammed to a stop, the force throwing him forward as the tires squealed on the pavement. Russ massaged his forehead where he'd hit the dashboard and glared at his driver. "What do you think you're doing?"

Victoria ignored him as she jerked the gearshift into reverse and rammed the accelerator to the floor. Stopping with another jerk, she cranked the steering wheel and turned, muttering under her breath.

Russ watched with a mixture of amusement and horror. The woman was a certifiable nut case. "Are we after someone in particular or did you just have a chocolate craving?"

She ignored him.

"Victoria, I'd suggest you tell me what's going on. I may be old and feeble, but I can still make you stop this car and talk to me."

His threats finally penetrated.

"I saw them. I know I did. It was the car my witness described as leaving the scene of the last robbery." She thumped her hand on the steering wheel in frustration. "Where could they have gone? There's nowhere out here to hide."

Russ felt the familiar rush of adrenaline course through his veins. "What car? You said the police don't have any witnesses."

"The police don't. I do." She let the car drift to a stop and glared at the surrounding countryside.

Rolling hills of farmland obscured the view quickly. And Russ knew from personal experience that these roads were worse than a maze, stopping, starting, and turning with no warning. The car could be close by, but they'd never find it—didn't even stand a chance.

He forced away the urge to take action, fought away the need to give pursuit, and directed his anger toward the woman sitting next to him. ''You haven't told anybody about this?''

He would strangle her. It was the only option. Superwoman was at it again, trying to single-handedly save the world. And she'd mess up another case for some other poor cop just like she'd done for him. Twice.

''I'll share my information. Don't get yourself in a snit. But I'll do it when I'm good and ready. The time isn't right yet.''

''And just when will it be right?''

A smile flashed across her lips. ''When I have the culprits dead to rights and can turn them over in a neat, tidy little package.''

Russ simply shook his head when she started driving again. All the facts Jayk had fed Russ now turned over in his mind as he worried over each detail. There had never been a car description, never any known witnesses. What did Victoria know? What had she found out?

After a few minutes, Russ made a decision. One that would undoubtedly get him in serious trouble with his unwanted keeper, but one that needed to be made.

Now he just needed to maneuver her into position. ''I do have one errand that needs to be taken care of. Would you mind driving me by the police station?''

Victoria shot him a suspicious glance, but he carefully kept his face bland. ''Why?''

''I need to fill out some papers. Something I've been putting off for weeks, but now that you've got me out of the house, I might as well get it done.''

She waited several heartbeats before agreeing. ''I'll wait in the car.''

''No problem. I shouldn't be gone more than a few minutes.'' Now he needed to be lucky enough to find Jayk in his office. Russ knew he was taking a chance, knew that Victoria would become even more impossible to work with when she found out, but he had to try.

Jayk would find a way to get Victoria inside. Russ knew he'd drag her out of the car if it became necessary.

Then, with luck and divine guidance, maybe they would get the information they needed— information that would lead to the arrest of the man who had shot Russ and left him broken and bleeding in the dark, garbage-filled alley.

Chapter Two

The familiar sounds of the station haunted him as Russ pushed his way through the double glass doors. A long hesitation halted his progress as he gathered the strength to continue. He didn't want to be here, didn't want to be reminded of the past.

Slowly, he made his way down the hall, knowing the feelings he stirred up might bring an end to the little sanity he had left. With a deep sense of relief, he made it to the detective division without seeing anyone he knew and edged toward the far end of the room.

After a sharp knock, he slipped inside the lieutenant's office before there was an answer. Jayk looked up with a trace of annoyance, then a smile broke over his face.

"Russ! Who finally managed to drag you out of your dungeon?"

Jayk stood, then hesitated, as if he wanted to help Russ into a chair, but knew better. Russ set his jaw and sat down without letting the pain show on his face. His ego had taken enough of a beating these past months; he couldn't tolerate having his friends and colleagues treat him like he was less than perfect. Even if it was true.

Jayk watched him carefully, then resumed his own seat. "How you doing, bud?"

Russ shrugged his shoulders. "Gettin' better. Any information yet?"

Running a hand over his face, Jayk winced. "You know we have no decent leads." He twisted a pen between his fingers. "There was another robbery."

"I heard. In fact, I've got a present for you. All it lacks is a pretty ribbon."

Jayk frowned.

"Victoria Stephens is poking around in your case. She's hinted that she has some leads you don't know about. And she's out in the parking lot now." The expression on Jayk's face gave Russ the satisfaction of realizing he was still of some use to the department, to someone.

"I can't help wishing that woman would move to another state, maybe even a new country. What did the Jackson Police Department ever do to deserve her?" Jayk gave a tired sigh. "She's messed up more cases than she's solved, but she manages to view herself as some kind of female Sherlock Holmes."

He shook his head, then grinned at Russ. "Do you think if you asked nicely she'd come see me?"

Russ grinned back, basking in the old, familiar comradery. "What do *you* think?"

Jayk picked up the phone and gave instructions to bring the woman to his office. "I thought the romance between the two of you was over."

"There was never a romance, Jayk. Just two people getting tangled up in each other's lives, two people who had no business even being in the same town together."

Jayk winked. "That's not how Kelly tells it."

"Kelly likes to build romance into my life. She's determined to return the matchmaking favor and can't understand why I won't grab the bait."

"Kelly tells me this time it will work."

Russ opened his mouth to protest, but a cold voice stopped him.

''You can let go of my arm. I'm not planning on going anywhere. At least not right this minute.''

Russ felt a flash of sympathy for the two uniformed officers who had brought her upstairs. At least they didn't appear to have any bruises or scratches, so maybe Victoria had behaved herself for once.

Jayk smiled and waved to a chair. ''Please, have a seat, Ms. Stephens. I hear there's some case information we need to talk about.''

Victoria shot a killing look at Russ, but slid into the chair. The uniforms left, obviously relieved to be free of their assignment.

''We have nothing to discuss, Lieutenant.'' Victoria crossed her legs and leaned back in the chair, the picture of innocence.

''You're nosing around in one of my cases. I'd say that gives us a lot to discuss.''

Victoria smiled and leaned forward. ''Tell you what. I'll share my information and you share yours. Maybe we can come up with a concrete lead if we pool our ideas.''

''You know I can't give out anything on a case that's active.''

''And you know I can't divulge my sources.''

Russ watched their battle of wills, afraid he already knew who would emerge victorious.

"Ms. Stephens, withholding information on an official police investigation is considered a crime—even if you are a reporter." Jayk propped his booted feet on the desk and glared at her.

"I'm not withholding information, Lieutenant. Everything I've got is pure speculation and I know you wouldn't want vague theories and rumors messing up your neat little facts."

Jayk sighed and glanced over at Russ. They both knew what had to be done, and both knew Russ was the one for the job. A look of understanding passed between the two men and Russ nodded his agreement.

Someone had to keep track of Victoria. The police didn't have the justification or the manpower to follow her around. Russ had nothing but time. And he finally had an excuse to make Victoria's life as miserable as she'd made his on several occasions in the past.

"You *will* share any new facts with us, right?" Jayk stood to end the interview.

"Of course, Lieutenant. You'll be the first to know." Victoria walked over to the doorway, then turned and smiled. "It really wasn't necessary to have an officer escort me up here, you know. All you had to do was ask nicely and I'd have been more than happy to talk with you."

Jayk returned the smile. "I just wanted to make certain you were safe, Ms. Stephens. Thank you for your time."

"Russ, I'll wait in the car while you finish up that paperwork. Don't be too long."

Russ watched her leave, his frustration digging at him. "Sorry, Jayk, but I was hoping you could intimidate her into saying something."

Jayk dropped a hand on Russ's shoulder. "It's okay. I'm willing to grasp at even the smallest straw right now. The evidence we have so far on the four robberies and the assault on you isn't enough to fill a one-page report." Jayk returned to his desk. "I feel a little guilty for saddling you with her. Think you can do it?"

"Stick with her?" Russ grinned. "It will be a pleasure. I've got nothing better to do and I owe her a few." He limped toward the door. "If she gets anything, I'll be so close I'll be able to hear her little reporter's pencil scratching down the words. Tell Kelly hello and I'll keep in touch. See ya, Jayk."

Russ worked his way down the hall, totally oblivious to the activity around him—the phones ringing, the people talking, the general chaos that was always a part of this station. He had a job to do, had to stick to Victoria like a burr to a saddle blanket.

And he was very good at sticking.

When he stepped out into the sunshine, he sucked in a deep breath of fresh air. The haunting memories of the past months faded to the background as his thoughts focused on what needed to be done.

He finally had a goal, a purpose. The thought filled him with an unexpected surge of energy, and he couldn't wait to get started.

As he approached the car, he watched the woman he was planning to become very well acquainted with. She pulled a brush through her gleaming blond hair, securing the long strands with a brightly colored scarf. When she turned the rearview mirror to touch up her makeup, she spotted him and immediately put away her things.

When he pulled open the car door, he saw fire in her blue eyes, the only outward sign of her anger. Russ slid into the seat, relishing the argument that was sure to follow. Adrenaline was humming through his system and he didn't want to lose the rush yet. It had been too long.

''That was dirty pool, Connor. Don't ever pull a stunt like that on me again.''

''Or what? You'll get even, I know. And you have the most devious ways of getting even of anyone I've ever met.'' He slammed the car door.

''But you're on to something,'' he continued, ''and I intend to find out what it is. Whoever committed those robberies also shot me. And I take that personally.'' He twisted in the seat, ignoring the twinges of pain.

''Get used to me, Victoria, because we're going to become very close for the next few weeks.'' He smiled, knowing the twist of his lips looked more like a threat.

She glared. Her mouth opened, then snapped shut again. Finally, she twisted the key in the ignition with a savage jerk and turned into the street. They'd driven three blocks before she managed an answer. ''I'll file harassment charges.''

Russ slipped his dark glasses on and faced her, knowing his face was a total blank. ''For what? Just because a man is spending time with you? Because a man is interested in you? I think it's time we get to know each other better. Maybe I'd even like to date you.'' He grinned. ''And I have nothing but time right now, so I can spend every waking minute savoring your company.''

''We know each other well enough. I don't want you around, Russ. Leave me alone.''

He leaned back in the seat. ''We'll stop for

dinner, then we can go to either your house or mine. But we *will* spend the evening together, Victoria. And we'll talk. Get used to the idea.''

Bullheaded, pompous, overbearing, arrogant... Victoria ran out of words bad enough to describe Russ Connor. His thick brown hair ruffled in the wind as she drove aimlessly through downtown Jackson. The dark glasses unsettled her, making it difficult for her to argue with him. If she could stare into his gray eyes when they had a disagreement, she could gauge him, figure out ways to best him. But the dark glasses masked everything from her.

She'd been on a mission of mercy, doing a favor for Kelly, an old friend from high school days. Victoria knew Russ, had gone her share of rounds with the man, had even dated him. Three times.

But she'd learned one thing very early in their relationship. Russ was dangerous. He could make her think about giving up her ambitions, about settling down, about having something resembling a normal life. And that was the last thing she wanted.

Now, because she'd allowed herself a weak moment, had actually felt sorry for the guy, he was back in her life. And he was intending to cling to her like a barnacle to the bottom of a boat.

She had to get rid of him. Tonight, she had a meeting with a new informant and she wasn't about to share her snitch with Russ.

Possibilities began swirling through her thoughts. She rejected each one until the perfect plan came to her. "Where did you want to eat?" she said aloud.

"Your choice. You're the driver."

Her mind ran through several choices. She needed someplace with easy access, someplace she was familiar with. The smile almost reached her lips as the perfect restaurant came to mind.

Russ had apparently forgotten just who he was dealing with.

When she pulled into the driveway, Russ nodded his approval. "I've always liked the steaks here. Good choice." His gaze ran through the parking lot.

She allowed him to take her elbow when they walked to the door. She tried to ignore the warm strength of his fingers. She even allowed him to secure their table. But when the waiter led the way across the room, she pulled away from Russ's disturbing touch.

"I need to go powder my nose," she equivocated. "I'll find you in a few minutes." Russ simply nodded and continued on into the dining room. Victoria resisted the urge to celebrate her getaway. The deed hadn't been done yet.

She slipped into the bathroom and waited a minute before going back to the door. When she peeked into the hallway, she almost screamed in frustration. Russ was lounging against the wall in the hallway. He couldn't possibly be standing there to protect her, which meant he suspected she might be up to something.

Somehow, the man had figured out her plan and was waiting to thwart her. He obviously didn't understand to what lengths she'd go to get rid of him. Once he learned that, he'd be forced to give up on the folly of following her around.

The bathroom window was small, but Victoria was confident she could slip through. Her figure had always been on the skinny side, which had saved her skin more than once. She pushed open the window and peered out. The drop to the ground wasn't more than six feet. The trick was getting in the right position to slide her legs out the window first so she landed on her feet instead of her head.

After a delicate balancing act on the small window ledge and a brief struggle with the old wooden frame, she had both feet pointed out the window and began wiggling her hips through. Thank goodness she'd had the sense to wear jeans today.

The sides of the window tightened around her until she felt the first traces of fear. What if she didn't fit? It would be totally embarrassing to be caught hanging halfway out like this. Russ would have a good laugh at her expense.

Again.

Pushing with her hands against the counter, she twisted once more until the window frame was around her waist. Just as she was getting ready to pull her arms through, unseen hands settled over her hips.

Victoria's scream bounced off the walls of the small bathroom.

Russ pulled her to the ground and set her on her feet. Her hands dropped to his broad shoulders for balance but she quickly jerked away when she saw the smirk on his lips.

"I must say, I enjoyed the view. But if you wanted to leave, all you had to do was say the word. This place is a little pricey and I don't mind eating somewhere else."

Anger surged through her. Pressing her lips together to staunch the flow of words begging to be released, she pushed his hands away. With a searing glare, she spun around, intending to beat him to the car and leave him standing in the parking lot. A jangling sound halted her.

"You forgot your purse. And your keys." Her car keys dangled from his fingers. She tried to snatch them away, but he pulled back. "I'll just carry these back to the car for you."

She hadn't planned to do it, had never even considered such an action in the past. But her hand balled into a fist and she put all her weight behind the swing. Russ seemed to move in slow motion as he reached up and grabbed her wrist. Using the force of her swing against her, he spun her around and cranked her arm up between her shoulder blades.

"Assaulting a police officer could get you jail time, lady."

His breath blew hot against her ear as she became very aware of the muscular chest she was pressed against. The anger warred with an unwelcome warmth as she struggled to free herself.

"Hold still, Victoria. I'll let you go as soon as you calm down."

She sucked in a deep breath, trying to force herself to stop, to think rationally, to react the way she should. But Russ upset her equilibrium, threw her off balance in a way no man had ever been allowed to before. She had to keep away from him.

She sagged against his hold, knowing the battle was lost before it could even be started.

''Good girl.'' Russ loosened his grip and stepped back.

''I'm not a girl!'' She swung again, and this time was able to connect with his shoulder before he could react.

Russ rubbed his shoulder and glared at her. ''You're not a lady either.''

That comment stung, but Victoria refused to let it show. In her line of work, it was often impossible to be a lady. And she suspected she'd forgotten how.

''Leave me alone, Russ. I don't want you around.'' She stalked away and climbed in the car with every intention of leaving him behind. But he still had the keys.

In the rearview mirror she watched his deliberate progress as he followed her, and her heart twisted. Russ had always been very active. Now he'd be hard pressed to catch a racing turtle.

The anger returned, but this time it was directed at the people who had dared hurt Russ. She'd find them, find them and make them pay for what they did. And get her story in the process. As he climbed into the seat beside her, she forced herself to remember the story. The story came first. That byline was all that counted in her life.

"I think round one goes to me, Victoria. What do you have planned next?"

He didn't smile. He just slipped on those infuriating mirrored glasses and turned to watch her.

"The keys?" She held out her hand, determined not to answer him.

He slipped the key into the ignition, then dropped his hand, still watching her.

A shiver traced a path up her spine. Frightened by her response, she twisted the key and let the engine roar to life. What next? It was his question, but she didn't have an answer for him.

"I'm going to take you home now, Russ. You shouldn't overdo it on your first day out of the house." She rushed the words, waiting for his protest. "Take it easy for the rest of the evening and I'll call you tomorrow. In fact, I promise to keep you updated on any new information I get. That way, you won't have to hurt your leg trying to keep up with me."

Pulling into traffic, she turned toward his house. "That's what I'll do. A daily report just for you. Since we're old friends and all. For old times' sake. . . . "

She let her words trail off, waiting for his response. But there was none. She sneaked a glance at him, but he was just sitting there, staring straight ahead.

''Do you want to call me each day or should I call you?''

Silence.

''I should probably call you, because I'm not always easy to contact. What's a good time of day for me to phone?''

He shifted his leg, but didn't answer her question.

When she pulled into his driveway, he still hadn't spoken and made no move to get out of the car.

''Do you need help?''

He waited for several heartbeats, then turned to her. ''I'm not that easy to get rid of. Unless you plan on throwing me out of this car, I'm going with you. Tonight, tomorrow, and for the rest of the month if that's what it takes. You can try to ditch me, but I'll find you, so let's just save each other a lot of trouble and work together.''

Victoria gripped the steering wheel so hard her knuckles turned white. She stared at her hands for a long moment. ''Never.''

''How long do you think we can sit in this driveway before someone notices? All night?

Two or three days? It's going to be a little uncomfortable tomorrow. It's supposed to get in the high nineties, isn't it?''

''Russ, you can't—''

''I can and I will. I have more stubbornness than you do, and much more at stake. Face it— we're working together.''

The steel in his voice convinced her. Telling the truth was her only other option.

''Look, I have a meeting tonight. It took me half an hour on the phone to get this guy to agree to see me. If he spots you and all your cop mannerisms, he'll run for certain. Let me meet him alone, okay? I'll get the information and we'll talk later.''

''No.''

''But—''

''Where are you meeting him?''

She sighed, knowing she'd lost another round. If she didn't work with him on this, he'd blunder into her meeting and spoil everything. ''A coffee shop on Fourth Street.'' Tomorrow was another day, another opportunity to lose him.

Russ nodded. ''I know the place. It has booths. Just drop me off there about a half hour before the meeting and I'll get the booth behind you. No one will even notice me.''

"Everyone will notice you. You're that kind of guy."

He raised his eyebrows. "A compliment, Victoria? Should I be flattered?"

She bit her lip, wanting to call the words back. But a female hadn't been born that was immune to Russ's innocent charm. Women and girls of all ages liked him.

And Victoria was afraid her feelings went beyond liking.

"Okay, Russ. I give up. Come to the meeting, listen in, and even take notes if you want. But stay out of my way."

He grinned and her insides melted. "Honey, I wouldn't consider getting in your way." He glanced at his watch. "What time is this rendezvous?"

"Seven o'clock."

"Good, then we still have time for dinner. There's a 7-Eleven down the street. We'll grab a hot dog and then get set up."

She couldn't help herself, couldn't have stopped her reaction if she'd thought to try. Returning his smile, she let the anger slip away. She wanted to enjoy his company, wanted to indulge herself. Just for a few hours, she'd allow it to happen. She'd have the entire night to get her armor back in place and to shore up her defenses. Then she could think of another way to get Russ Connor out of her life and off of her case.

"You sure know how to show a girl a good time. Hot dogs at 7-Eleven. Does that impress all your dates, or just the high-class ones?"

"Just the high-class ones, Victoria. And especially you."

She basked in the lopsided compliment as she backed out of the driveway. She'd been planning to demand steak with all the trimmings, just to make him pay a big food bill. But suddenly, that hot dog sounded very tempting.

Chapter Three

The sigh escaped more loudly than he intended as he eased onto the cracked upholstery of the booth. His leg was reminding him of the abuse he'd placed on it today. After months of little more exercise than pacing the floor in his small house, one day of keeping up with Victoria was more than he was in shape for.

The waitress took his order for coffee and pie as Russ sat back to wait, relishing the anticipation curling through him. He felt alive again, felt on the edge, knowing anything could happen. Victoria might very well have saved his sanity, but he'd never tell her that. When this was over he'd probably owe her a big debt of gratitude.

He hated owing anyone anything.

When the pie arrived, Russ took a small forkful, savoring the burst of flavors across his tongue. He'd been living on stale bread and luncheon meat since his last operation, lacking the drive to plan even a simple meal. Yet at one time, eating had ranked high on his list of favorite pastimes.

His treat was almost half finished before Victoria walked in and took a seat in the booth behind him. His senses shifted to full alert as the minutes ticked slowly past.

Just as he was about to turn around and tell Victoria her snitch wasn't going to show, a small man with hard eyes pulled open the door. Russ looked him over carefully and knew he'd been right in insisting on being here. Victoria was in way over her head and didn't even have the sense to know it.

The man paused beside her table. "Ma'am?"

The conversation that followed was everything Russ had expected it to be. The stranger demanded money, Victoria demanded information, and neither got what they wanted. Victoria's harsh protest when the man turned to leave brought Russ out of the booth.

The stranger had her purse and her notebook in his hands, but Victoria was still clutching the long strap of her purse, trying to stop him.

Russ almost grinned, knowing she would hang on to that strap forever if he didn't intervene.

The stranger took a step back toward Russ and Russ simply twisted his cane between the man's legs. With just the right leverage, the man fell to the floor in a heap. Russ rolled him over, twisted an arm behind his back, and grinned at his reluctant partner.

"Call the police, honey. This guy's got some explaining to do."

"But he's—"

"Vicky." The warning note in his voice was all that was needed. She pressed her lips together and turned away.

The throbbing pain in his leg increased with each passing minute as he helped Victoria deal with the uniforms. But he refused to admit his weakness, even to himself. When they finally reached the car, he sank into the seat with a deep sigh of relief.

Victoria tossed her purse into the backseat and slammed the car door. Her hands clenched the steering wheel and Russ suspected she was wishing it was his neck her fingers were wrapped around. "Don't ever do that to me again."

He rolled his head on the headrest until he was facing her. Anger pinched her lips and he suddenly found himself fighting the urge to kiss her until she relaxed, which proved just how tired he really was. "Do what? Save your hide? Sorry, I thought I was helping."

"I can handle myself, Connor."

"Yeah, right. Should I have waited until the guy dragged you out the door, or just let him take you along with the purse?"

She jammed the keys into the ignition. "Cute. Real cute."

She froze when he stroked his fingers down the side of her face. An unexpected wave of tenderness rolled through him and for once, he let himself react to it. "I don't want to see you hurt, Victoria."

She trembled, then pulled ever so slightly out of his reach. "Don't."

He smiled, knowing he was starting to break through the walls she'd so efficiently erected between them. "Don't what?"

"Don't be nice to me. I hate it when you're nice to me." Her tone was angry, defiant.

"Why?" The simple question echoed between them for a long minute.

"Because I don't want it. I don't want to care about you. And if you're nice to me, I will. I can't let that happen, Russ."

Russ felt a stab of disappointment when she started the car. He didn't want the evening to end yet, wasn't ready to leave Victoria. But he couldn't think of one single thing to stop her determined journey toward his house.

The flashing neon of a local drugstore came into view, bringing the inspiration he needed. "Could we make just one stop? I need to get some kind of painkiller."

"Did you hurt yourself at the café?"

"No. I'm just tired. Not used to this much excitement."

"Don't you have something from the doctor?"

He shook his head, not willing to admit the battle he'd fought with the temptation of taking more and more painkillers. Because not only had the drugs numbed his physical pain, but they'd numbed his mind. The blessed relief from worrying about his future had beckoned one too many times and he'd flushed the little white pills down the toilet.

He dawdled in the far aisle of the drugstore, stalling, trying to think of another excuse to extend their evening. Dinner hadn't worked out the way he'd planned and he wasn't up to much else. He didn't think Victoria would consent to a quiet game of cards at the house either.

There had to be a way to keep her around for a little bit longer. He didn't want the dark, quiet night closing in on him just yet. With the nighttime came the fears and he wasn't ready to face them. He wasn't strong enough this time.

His cane clanked against the shelving and Russ smiled. He wasn't above using his weakened state to get a little attention from Victoria. She had a soft spot for him; he was certain of it. Otherwise, she wouldn't have stopped by to visit him this morning, no matter what arguments Kelly had used.

He grabbed a bottle of generic aspirin and thought back on their day as he headed for the cash register. One cruel twist of fate had probably taken his career from him. But another unexpected twist had thrown Victoria into his life and given him something to live for again.

Suddenly, Russ couldn't wait for tomorrow—tomorrow when he could play cat and mouse with a very lovely lady. Tomorrow, when he could have a second chance at living again, a chance he'd foolishly almost thrown away.

Victoria was tapping an impatient beat on the steering wheel when he finally came out. As he slid into the seat, he couldn't resist tormenting her. "Home, James."

She glared at him, but started to back out of the parking space. When she slammed on the brakes, he almost hit his head on the dashboard. Again. The woman was more hazardous to his health than all his years of police work had ever been.

"Now what?" He tried to keep the aggravation out of his voice, but suspected he'd failed.

"That car. . . . "

Russ groaned, seeing his plans for some quiet time with her going up in a puff of smoke because of her overactive imagination.

"The colors aren't quite right, but it could pass for the vehicle I'm looking for." She jammed the car into gear and squealed the tires as she darted out of the parking lot.

"That's it, be careful and just sneak up on them real quiet-like. They'll never know you're behind them with all this darkness." He couldn't keep the sarcasm from his voice.

"Shut up, Russ. I'm trying to concentrate." The car leaned hard as she took the corner a little too fast.

"And *I'm* trying to survive." He grabbed the dashboard with one hand while groping for the seat belt with the other. "Vicky, just get the license number and we'll call Jayk."

"No way. This is *my* information."

"Well, when you catch them, what are you going to do with them? I can't see the two of us holding off a carload of desperadoes with my cane and your purse until the posse arrives.''

''I don't know yet, but I'm sure something will come to me. It always does when I need it.''

The car ahead of them pushed through a yellow light and Victoria darted through on a red. A car horn sounded behind them, but she ignored it, her attention totally on the vehicle in front of them.

''They've made us. I'll bet they try to run now.'' Excitement laced her voice.

''Vicky, you've watched too many movies. Just let me get the license number, then back off.'' His fingers dug deeper into the dashboard and he wondered if he dared release his grip long enough to write anything down.

Probably not.

Cutting a corner too closely, Victoria bounced over the curb without slowing down. Russ considered turning off the motor and yanking the keys from the ignition, but had no doubt she'd find a way to continue the chase. At least in the car, she was where he could keep an eye on her.

Without warning, the car in front of them slowed, then changed lanes. As they pulled closer, Russ quickly memorized the license number, then mumbled a little prayer for good measure. It might not help, but it certainly wouldn't hurt.

Victoria pulled up beside the car, trying to sneak a subtle peak at the driver. When the driver leaned out the window to speak, Victoria jumped and tried to look interested in something in the distance.

"You wanna drag, honey?" A devilish twinkle lit faded blue eyes as the driver gunned the motor in a defiant show of power.

Russ tried not to laugh, certain Victoria would never forgive him, but his mirth came out in a hearty chuckle that almost drowned out Victoria's embarrassed refusal to race down the street.

The white-haired lady in the other car frowned in disappointment. "I haven't been able to scare up a good race yet tonight. Too bad. You look like you could give me a real run for my money."

The light switched to green and their would-be opponent left two stripes of rubber on the pavement, waggling her fingers out the window in a cheery good-bye.

"You're right, Vicky. She looks dangerous. I have the license number and we can call it in from the next pay phone. I'm sure the police can pick her up yet tonight and the case will be solved by morning."

"Shut up, Russ." Victoria pulled over to the curb and stopped, leaning her head against the steering wheel. "And don't call me Vicky."

"But this could be the big break you're looking for. I've heard of these gangs of little old ladies. They can't live on their retirement pensions, so they turn to crime. A jewelry store heist would be just the thing for such a sweet-looking suspect."

He saw her make a fist, saw her swing, but didn't try to deflect it. She smacked him in the chest, causing his laughter to come out a little wheezy. But he was having too much fun to cease his teasing.

"There's a phone—"

"One more word out of you, Connor, and you can walk home." She stared through the windshield, but he didn't need to see her eyes to know she was furious because he'd been there to witness her mistake.

"But that's over two miles." He brushed a hand over his mouth, trying to muffle the grin that pulled at his lips.

"Consider it physical therapy."

He chuckled. "I'll be good. Just take me home and I won't say another word."

The remainder of the drive was made in the promised silence. Russ felt the thrill of action chasing through his system and hoped this particular case with Victoria didn't wrap up too quickly.

As badly as he wanted to hang the guys who shot him, Russ needed Victoria in his life right now. He needed the excitement and anticipation she offered him. Because being with this woman excited him in ways he refused to even consider.

When they stopped in front of his house, he eyed the uneven surface of his driveway and suppressed his satisfaction. Payback time was at hand.

"Do you need help?" Victoria frowned at him.

"I've kept up with you so far today. I think I can stagger into the house before I collapse."

"Good night, Russ. And don't bother to chase after me tomorrow. I'll be in the field all day and you won't know where to look for me."

Russ grinned. "You'd be surprised at what I know." He eased from the car, taking three steps before stumbling and letting himself twist to the ground with an exaggerated groan.

"Russ!" She was out of the car and at his side before he could even make certain he was arranged in a properly pitiful position. "Are you okay?"

He breathed in heavily. "Yeah, I think so. I

just tripped on the cracked cement.'' He threw in another groan for good measure as she stroked his face and hovered. What he wouldn't give for his dark glasses now. He was no actor, but hopefully the night shadows were thick enough to conceal any mistakes he made.

''Do I need to call an ambulance?''

''No.'' His protest came too quickly. ''I'm fine. Just help me inside and I'll go to bed. Rest is still the best medicine.''

She put an arm around him and helped him to a sitting position. He turned his face and breathed in the clean scent of her hair, resisting the urge to pull her mouth to his for a kiss.

Tugging and pulling, she tried to help him to his feet, but Russ just sat there. ''A little help on your part wouldn't hurt, buster.''

''Okay.'' He tried to infuse a weakness in his voice and knew he'd succeeded when her glare turned to worry. Then her eyes narrowed.

''You wouldn't be faking this, would you? Is this your sick way of getting even?''

''Victoria, would I do a thing like that to you?'' He plastered what he hoped was an innocent expression on his face.

''Yes, you would.'' She braced herself. ''Now help me to get you to your feet so we can go inside. I don't want to put on a show for your neighbors.''

"Mrs. Pastor needs the excitement. And she's always watching out the front window. Maybe we should give her something to get her heart started?" He turned his face toward hers and puckered his lips.

When she let go of him, he almost cracked his head on the driveway. "Hey, I was only joking."

"You're always joking, Russ." She started around the front of the car. "Maybe Mrs. Pastor will help you inside. If not, the night's supposed to be warm, so it won't hurt you to sleep right where you are. Maybe the hard concrete will put you in touch with reality."

He thrust out his lower lip and widened his eyes. "You don't love me anymore?"

"You're impossible." She braced her hands on her hips as a heavy sigh escaped her. "I can't leave you out here any more than I could kick the neighbor's yapping little poodle." As she returned to his side, she wagged a finger in his face. "Behave. My good Samaritan urges can only be stretched so far."

"Yes, ma'am," Russ answered meekly. Even he knew when he'd pushed the limits far enough. He'd wait until they got inside before tormenting her a little further.

Their trip up the three small steps was long and laborious. Russ made certain he put a heavy weight on her, figuring it was a small enough payback for the car ride that had taken at least three years off his life. She braced him against the wall and waited while he fumbled with his keys. Finally she snatched the key chain from his hand and inserted the key into the lock, muttering in her irritation.

When the door swung open, she started to turn away.

''I'm going to need help getting undressed.''

Her anger seemed to vibrate the air around them. ''No, you don't, Russ. Trust me, you don't want any more help from me. Because I'm fast reaching the point where I may have to hurt you just to make myself feel better.''

''You'd never hurt a fly. You forget, I've seen your softer side.'' He dared to touch his finger to her cheek. ''You're a pussycat underneath all that anger.''

She blinked and he could tell memories of their three dates were sifting through her thoughts. He knew the exact moment when she remembered the disastrous rescue of the duckling and the fuss she'd raised until he'd made certain it was taken care of.

''It wasn't my fault the ice was too thin and you fell into the lake.''

''Yes, it was. Thank goodness the lake was only two feet deep. You still owe me for that one. Please just help me into the bedroom. I'll try to get undressed by myself.'' He sighed dramatically. ''I just hope I don't hurt my leg any more than I already have. The doctor won't be happy.''

Victoria groaned and started forward. ''You win.'' Her arm settled around his waist.

Together, they crossed the living room floor, dodging the clutter he'd failed to pick up for too long. When they finally reached the bedroom, he eased onto the bed with a sigh of relief. The playacting was becoming easier by the moment. His leg had started to throb with a vengeance.

''I'll . . . uh . . . wait in the living room while you get undressed.'' She hesitated at the door. ''Just to make sure you're all right.''

He wanted to ask her to help him into his pajamas, but he didn't wear any. After slipping his jeans off, he leaned against the headboard. Leaving his T-shirt on to spare her modesty, he pulled the covers over his bare legs. ''I'm all snuggled in, Victoria. Thanks,'' he called.

A long moment passed, then the door cracked open and she peeked inside. ''Can I get you anything? A drink or something?''

He grinned. ''How about a good-night kiss?''

Her lips clamped together. ''I don't think so.''

''Will you sing me to sleep?''

''In your dreams, bud.''

''Well, it sort of would be in my dreams if I were sleeping, wouldn't it?''

She came further into the room, glaring down at him. ''Are you always this impossible?''

''Yes.'' He scooted down in the bed, settling his head on the pillow.

Her lips twitched and she finally returned his smile. ''I guess I knew that.''

She leaned over him and pulled the blanket under his chin, just like his mother used to. When she started to pull away, Russ brushed a strand of hair from her face, but kept a gentle grip on one soft curl. ''Thanks, Victoria.''

''Any time, macho man.'' She stood and went to the doorway before pausing. ''I suppose I'll be seeing you first thing in the morning?''

''Why don't we make it easy and you can pick me up on your way to work?''

''I'll never make it easy for you, Connor.'' She threw a grin over her shoulder before retreating. ''You'll have to find your own way to follow me around. I'm not going to help you.''

His sigh filled the room as she snapped off the light. His leg was hurting, but it had felt stronger than ever tonight. Maybe just the excitement of living again was the best medicine he could have. Tomorrow, he'd leave the cane at home. Maybe then, Victoria would view him as a viable accomplice.

Maybe then, she would see him as a man rather than as a sparring partner.

Chapter Four

"Kelly, you've got to do something about him."

"About who?" Kelly wiped five-year-old Tammy's nose, then sent her on her way with a gentle swat on her bottom.

"Russ. He was your partner, he is *your* friend, so you've got to stop him." Victoria suspected she was being unreasonable in asking, but she was desperate. After one sleepless night, she knew she had to get Russ Connor out of her life.

Fast. Before she asked him to stay.

"Stopping Russ comes in second only to trying to halt a charging elephant." Kelly laughed. "How did you manage to lose him today?"

51

"I didn't go into the office. I came straight here, hoping he'd check at work and then start driving around town looking for me." She tapped her fingers on the table. "Maybe I should call in sick tomorrow, then disappear somewhere else."

"Good plan. But Russ has the nose of a bloodhound, or else he's psychic, because he's always found people and things no one else could." Kelly set a jar of strained carrots in a pan of water to warm. "Don't underestimate him."

Victoria had made the mistake once of underestimating Russ. She'd been lonely and Russ was good company. He made her laugh. She'd thought she could just be friends with him, just spend time talking and sharing. Never again would she make such a dangerous error in judgment.

She resorted to pleading with her friend. "Talk to him—please. I can't have him following me around every day. The man thinks he's going to get a lead on this case through me and I won't let him scare off another informant." She stopped, pursing her lips. "I know that's why that guy wouldn't talk to me last night. Somehow, he sensed Russ, knew someone else was listening."

Victoria stopped, almost afraid to say what

was on her mind. Because if she put the feeling into words, if she allowed herself more than vague thoughts in the dark of night, it held a chance of coming true. "Besides, he's dangerous."

"Who? The informant you met last night?"

"No, Russ."

Kelly sat down beside her friend, a worried frown creasing her forehead. "Has the injury changed him? Is he getting . . . violent?"

It was Victoria's turn to laugh, but the sound held little amusement. "No, he's far from violent. He's kind, gentle, caring, and far too nice in an arrogant, macho sort of way." She dropped her head into her hands. "The man drives me nuts."

The man could drive her to forget everything she'd learned watching her own mother struggling to juggle work and family.

All traces of Kelly's sympathy vanished. "Is that all?"

"Kelly!"

"So he's dangerous to your freedom? He threatens that perfect little life you've mapped out for yourself?"

"Yes." Victoria's mouth tightened as she was forced to admit the truth. She was attracted to Russ, but she didn't want to be.

Kelly studied her friend for a long moment.

"Look, there's one thing I learned about Russ in working with him for two years. No one can tell him to do anything. He has to be convinced that whatever is happening is his idea, and then he'll go for it." She tapped her finger against her lips. "You need to distract him, send him on some wild goose chase."

Hope shined in Victoria's eyes. "You mean give him a false lead or something?" It sounded so simple the way Kelly said it. But Victoria knew nothing with Russ would ever be considered easy.

Kelly shrugged. "It might work. If you make it complicated enough, you could be rid of him for several days." She snapped her fingers. "I know, tell him you've got some information you need him to follow up on. Because you're too busy on another story. You're a writer; make something up. Maybe even send him out of town to find some unknown person."

"Is China too far away?"

Kelly's laughter filled the room. "He might be a little suspicious about that. Make it ten miles down the road, not the other side of the world. I don't think these jewel thieves would travel that far."

"After all the things I said to him yesterday, I think he'd be suspicious if I offered to let him help at all. But I'll think of something. I have to.''

The baby started fussing and Victoria eagerly reached for the sweet-smelling bundle. ''You've given me hope, Kelly. This case can't drag on forever.'' And when it was over, she'd never have to see him again. A little twinge of loneliness marred her determination, but she pushed it away.

To distract herself, Victoria kissed Charles on the cheek and played with the baby's toes. She knew the sooner she forced Russ Connor out of her life, the better off she'd be.

The screen door creaked open and the object of her worries unexpectedly appeared in the kitchen. Victoria swallowed, trying to bury the mixture of dread and pleasure she felt at seeing him again.

''Russ, what brings you way out here?'' Kelly took the baby from her friend and tucked him into the crook of her arm for his morning snack.

''First of all, it's been way too long since I saw my godson and second, I need to keep an eye on Ms. Supersleuth here.'' Russ crossed the room slowly, his limp almost painful to watch, and tickled the underside of Charles's chin.

The baby gurgled strained carrots and Kelly

patiently wiped away the mess. Russ nodded his approval. ''That's my boy. Hold out for the good stuff. Tell her you want steak and potatoes next time.''

''Russ, don't corrupt him just yet. Let the boy grow some teeth, maybe get to the ripe old age of three or four, before you give him ideas.''

''Hey, he's got to have a head start just to keep ahead of the women these days. They're getting a little too smart for their own good.'' With a grin, he turned to Victoria. '' 'Morning, partner. Ready to go to work?''

His smile sent a tingle through Victoria, her anger at the uncontrolled response making her voice sharper than she'd intended. ''How did you find me?''

She glared at him, wondering if he'd managed to attach one of those high-tech tracking devices to her car when she wasn't looking.

Russ tapped his nose. ''Good police work and an unfailing instinct for how your devious little mind works.''

Kelly laughed. ''In other words, you came looking for a free breakfast and just happened to stumble onto your quarry.''

''Kelly, you wound me. I hit the drive-through bright and early this morning for one of those egg things. But I wouldn't object to a morning snack if you're offering.'' His hopeful expression melted even Victoria's frustration.

"I'm not, but there's fresh coffee and chocolate-chip cookies in the cookie jar. Unless Jimmy ate them all last night.''

Victoria watched Russ make his way across the room, trying not to acknowledge the deep hunger he ignited in her. He made her want certain things—long-term things—she'd convinced herself she couldn't have if she wanted a successful career.

"Well, these teenage boys do need their fuel,'' Russ told Kelly, referring to her thirteen-year-old brother, Jimmy. His hand delving deep into the jar, Russ turned back to Kelly. "How's the life of the nonworking mother treating you?''

"I love it. Kids are a much bigger challenge than police work and it's such a luxury not to have to go into work every day.''

"Think you'll ever go back to it?'' He poured a cup of coffee, adding a large spoonful of sugar.

"Not as long as I can convince Jayk we need to have more kids. This house can hold a lot more than we've got.''

Victoria felt a sharp twinge of jealousy. She had made a conscious choice of career over wife and family, but sometimes—just once in a while—she wished it could be different. She wished she could have it all. Because she could see how happy Kelly was, and longed for the same contentment in her own life.

The thrill of meeting deadlines, interviewing witnesses, and covering catastrophes was her lifeblood. But her apartment grew awfully quiet at times, and if she didn't make a distinct effort to get busy, the silence closed in, threatening to suffocate her.

She watched as Russ counted the chips in his cookie. "I thought you weren't allowed to drive a car yet. And shouldn't you be using your cane?" Victoria glared at him, angry that he'd made her remember everything she was missing in her life.

Russ took a gulp of coffee. "The doctor doesn't know how my leg feels as well as I do. It'll be okay. Besides, I can't keep up with you with that third leg trailing me."

"But why risk injuring yourself just to make my life miserable? Won't you be delaying your chance to go back to work?" She had to find an argument that would deter him from his self-appointed mission.

It was little more than a flicker in his eyes, but Victoria saw the pain, the fear, and regretted her tactics. She wanted to be rid of him, but she didn't want to cause him any more anguish. "If you rested like you're supposed to rather than trailing after me, you'd heal faster."

His sudden grin was filled with the devil. "Why, Victoria, you make it sound like I'm chasing after you. I told you I'd meet you today to help with your investigation and that's just what I'm doing. Unless you plan to pick a fight with another innocent bystander, it shouldn't be too strenuous for me."

Kelly raised an eyebrow as she turned to look at Victoria. "Have you taken up street brawling without telling me?"

"Russ is exaggerating. A man, my informant, tried to take my purse. I just needed a little . . . help in getting it back."

Kelly closed her eyes and shook her head.

Tammy burst into the room and headed straight for Russ's arms. "Uncle Russ!" She jumped up, wrapping her legs around his. Fortunately, Russ was used to the maneuver and caught her under the arms before she could tumble to the floor.

"How's my little darlin' today?"

"Mommy won't let me go outside 'cause I got the snuffles." Tammy threw her arms around his neck. "You make her change her mind so I can go play with Red. He misses me."

Russ threw a helpless look at Kelly, who simply smiled.

"You got yourself into this mess by indulging her so many times, Russ, so you get yourself out. But she can't go outside until her nose quits dripping like a faucet." Tammy punctuated Kelly's warning with a loud sniffle.

Russ sat Tammy on the countertop and bent until he was eye level with her. "Did you know that dogs can catch colds too?" Tammy watched him with wide eyes. "And you wouldn't want poor old Red to feel as bad as you do, now would you?"

Tammy stared at him for a long moment. "I won't breathe on him. 'Sides, I don't feel bad, I just sound terrible."

Russ squirmed. "But you can still give your germs to Red, so you'd better stay in for now. He hasn't mastered the technique of blowing his nose with one of those little bitty tissues yet."

Tammy pushed her lower lip out in an exaggerated pout. "You're mean."

Russ let his gaze meet with Victoria's. "Yeah, I've been told that before. But you'll get over it. Now, why don't you draw me one of your special pictures before I have to leave?"

Her pout forgotten, Tammy ran to her room for her crayons.

Victoria watched the exchange with a strange heaviness surrounding her heart. Russ was wonderful with kids. He deserved to be a father. She wanted a chance to develop that same ease around kids, especially Kelly's. In fact, Victoria was Tammy's godmother. That was as close as she'd allow herself to get to being a mother.

Kelly had managed to give up her much-loved career for family and still find happiness. Victoria knew she couldn't do the same. It wasn't fair to expect kids to grow up while one or both parents pursued other dreams and left their children to the mercies of a long string of baby-sitters.

Russ glanced at Victoria. "Well, boss, are you just about done wasting time so we can get back to work and wrap this case up?"

Victoria grabbed her purse, kissed Charles on the only clean skin on his face, and silently pleaded with Kelly to aid and abet her escape. Kelly pursed her lips, looking like she wanted to argue, but she finally nodded her agreement.

Kelly lifted the baby from the high chair. "Russ, take care of Charles for a minute while I get a washcloth." She stuffed the sticky baby into his arms before he could respond.

As soon as Kelly left the room, Victoria smiled at Russ. ''I've got to run. I have an appointment.''

She waggled her fingers in his direction and almost laughed at the frustration on his face as he struggled to hold the baby securely, yet keep strained carrots off his shirt.

When Charles's orange-covered hand grabbed the soft blue shirt and left a gooey trail down the front, Victoria silently thanked Kelly. Her friend had bought plenty of time for Victoria to get some work done, then disappear again. Because now Russ would have to go home and change clothes before bothering her again.

''See you around, macho man.'' She laughed quietly at his muttered curses, closing off the sound of his anger with a defiant slam of her car door.

The man might be able to outsmart one woman, maybe even two women on a good day, but add a baby to the formula and he was sunk every time.

Charles tugged on Russ's shirt and gurgled happily. Russ's anger dissolved when he looked down into the toothless smile the baby bestowed on him. Russ loved the kid and held a secret hope he could someday have several children of his own. But since his future had been drastically changed by one very small bullet, he wasn't certain he had anything left to offer that special woman when he found her.

"Oh, Russ, I'm so sorry." Kelly came back into the room and took the baby from him.

Russ was certain he saw her lips twitch with the urge to smile, but Kelly had always occupied a soft spot in his heart and he couldn't whip up a decent anger. She swiped at his shirt, smearing the carrots in deeper, until he caught her wrist to still her efforts.

"Traitor."

She glanced up, her guilt reflected in her eyes. "For what? Asking you to hold Charles?"

"You know what I mean. Luckily, I know right where to look for her." He leaned forward and kissed the baby on the top of the head. "Take care of her, sport." When he reached for the screen door, Kelly's words stopped him.

"Go easy on her, Russ."

He turned to stare at her in disbelief. "*Me* go easy on *her*?"

Kelly nodded. "She's had a rough time of it. Don't make life too difficult for her."

Russ laughed. "I think you'd better tell her to go easy on me. I'm the wounded one, remember?"

He paused as he remembered just who had started this entire fiasco. ''What the devil made you decide I needed her in my life anyway? What did I ever do to you?''

''Maybe you need each other more than you think.''

''I need that woman like I need another bullet in my leg.'' With a wave, he left, hoping he really did know where Victoria was going.

He mulled over Kelly's warning as he drove. He actually knew very little about Victoria's life, her childhood. Three dates didn't give a man much time to know a woman's past pain. But in that time, he had learned that Victoria was single-minded about her career and that no one got in her way for long.

And that meant it was very stupid for him to even let the thought of a relationship enter his mind. He was too old to be thinking of a just-friends type of thing. He needed more from the woman in his life. But now he had nothing to offer in return.

When he found Victoria, it wasn't where he thought she'd be and not nearly as quickly as he'd hoped to. Certain she had to go to her office sometime during the day, he'd checked there first. But they hadn't seen her. His frustration grew as he checked the scene of each robbery, hoping she was interviewing witnesses. When he did finally spot her, it was purely by accident.

He'd taken a wrong turn and ended up in an older section of town, one of those areas very few nonresidents went through after dark. When he caught a glimpse of a bright blue blouse, he refused to believe she'd be here. Alone. But her swinging walk confirmed his suspicions and his jaw tightened with an anger he hoped she had the sense to see and respect.

He twisted the steering wheel, struggling to pump the break with his left foot so he could protect his weak leg. Rolling down the window, he coasted to a stop a few feet in front of her.

"Why aren't you in your office?"

She smiled at him, but there was no welcome in her look. "I work in the field most of the time. Why aren't you at home, resting?"

He ignored her question. "Meeting another one of your informants?"

She sighed. "What I'm doing has nothing to do with your case. Trust me, Russ. I was working on an entirely different story."

"Trust?" His voice cracked over a word he'd never use in the same breath as her name. "I should trust a devious woman like you?"

She glared her answer.

"Get in the car before you get hurt," he ordered.

She stopped, looked carefully around, then frowned at Russ. "What's going to hurt me? I don't see anything dangerous."

"You'd better start showing some sense." He pulled himself from the car and stood in front of her.

"As you can see, I'm just fine." She brushed past him. "And I have work to do."

"Your work is done in this neighborhood." He grabbed her arm to stop her, but with a quick twist she was free of him.

Suddenly, Russ realized he would accomplish nothing with that attitude. Abruptly, he smiled and stepped back to lean against the car, prepared to fight dirty to get her out of here. "I'll buy you an ice-cream cone."

He saw her hesitate and had to force back his triumph. Victoria's weakness for ice cream had become very apparent to him by the end of their first date.

He dangled the image of the bribe in front of her like a juicy carrot. "French vanilla with chocolate sprinkles and nuts on top? Maybe a cherry?"

She licked her lips and swallowed, hard.

"In a waffle cone?"

She groaned. "You don't play fair, Connor.'' She glanced at her watch. ''Okay, it's lunchtime anyway. Where do you want to meet?''

''Why don't you just ride with me?'' He wanted her corralled, close by, where he could have a small measure of control.

''As you said, this is a dangerous neighborhood. I won't leave my car here, unattended. There'd be very little of it left when I came back.''

He wasn't willing to give up so easily. ''Well, let me drive you to your car, then I'll follow you. You pick the spot.''

''Thanks, but I'll walk. Think you can keep up?''

He'd keep up, all right. He'd do more than keep up. As she walked away, he admired the gentle sway of her hips, letting himself be totally distracted from his mission for a few precious seconds.

When she turned the corner, he jerked away from the car and got inside. He drove around the corner and slammed on the brakes, disbelief overriding the stab of pain in his leg.

Victoria stood on the curb, trying to wrestle a hubcap away from a scruffy boy. They tugged back and forth like two dogs fighting over an old sock. Russ got out and yelled at the kid, who jumped away and ran down the alley.

Victoria stood shaking her hand, sticking two fingers in her mouth as a wince of pain crossed her face.

"Are you all right?" He moved closer.

"Brat. He almost succeeded in pulling my fingers off." She held out her hand for his inspection. Dark red grooves marred her fingertips where she'd been clinging to the hubcap.

Russ resisted the urge to kiss her hand, to try to make the hurt go away. Just barely. Victoria was drawing him closer every minute he spent with her. Maybe it was time to give up. Maybe it was time to tell Jayk he couldn't follow Victoria the way they'd planned.

His jaw tightened. Because after less than twenty-four hours, she'd already managed to make him hopping mad and weak with wanting. He shook his head, trying to shake some sense into himself. Again, he looked at her fingers.

"Couldn't you just let him have that thing?"

"At twenty-five dollars a hubcap? No way."

He chuckled and shook his head. "Aw, sweet lady, what am I going to do with you?"

She dropped her hand and returned his smile. "Feed me ice cream?"

"Of course. Such bravery definitely deserves a reward.'' Russ took the hubcap from her hand and snapped it back into place. Then he held her car door open with a flourish and waited until she was securely inside. ''Lead on, Macduff.''

When she started her engine, he got back into his own car. She was leading him, all right. Leading him into uncharted waters and into even deeper trouble. Trouble he wasn't certain he was ready to have in his life. But did he have any choice?

Chapter Five

Victoria tapped her finger against her lips while she studied the menu on the wall. "I can't decide what to have."

Russ resisted the urge to sigh in frustration. She was doing this deliberately. "How about the same thing you always have—vanilla with chocolate sprinkles and nuts?"

"That was what I was having a few years ago. Maybe my tastes have changed." She pursed her lips. "The strawberry looks good, but then so does the chocolate mint." She pointed to a purple swirled concoction. "May I have a taste of that one?"

The clerk scooped out a small spoonful and handed it to Victoria. She tasted it, rolled it around on her tongue like a fine wine, then shook her head. ''No, that's not what I want.'' Pointing to another flavor, she asked for a second taste.

Russ ground his teeth at her delaying tactics. He wanted to get back to work. He needed to take some action and do something positive. Baby-sitting Victoria was not on his list of most-wanted things to do today. But then again, he admitted with a wry grin, he'd appointed himself her protector over her protests, so he probably had nothing to complain about.

''I guess I'll have vanilla with chocolate sprinkles and nuts.''

When Russ shook his head, she glared at him. She didn't wait while he paid for her treat, just sailed out the door and leaned against the brick wall. Slowly, he followed, wondering just how he should respond. Then he realized that a response, any response, was just what she was looking for. His best strategy was to ignore the entire incident. With a carefully placed smile, he walked over to a sidewalk table and pulled out a chair for her.

''Nice shirt.'' She slipped into her seat.

Russ let his hand hover over her blond hair before stepping back. As he walked around the table he remembered how soft the silky strands used to feel to his touch, how he'd loved to bury his fingers in the thick length. Reluctantly, he sat across from her, slipping on his sunglasses to cut the glare of the sun. "A gift from baby Charles. I've been too busy chasing after you to go home and change."

"I didn't ask you to follow me." She tasted the ice cream, her lips curving into a satisfied smile.

"But you got yourself in trouble and I had to bail you out." He was proud of the way he refrained from adding the "again" he wanted to use.

"I was doing fine without you. I almost had that hubcap back and then I'd have dealt with the kid."

"By hitting him over the head with that little piece of metal, I suppose."

Victoria shrugged. "It might have worked. But I like to use a little more finesse than that. I took a self-defense course once that taught some unique methods of stopping someone." Slowly, she rotated the cone, as if she were planning her attack on it.

"I can just imagine." He shuddered and closed his eyes, slightly terrified by the idea of Victoria attacking anyone. Somehow, he knew she'd win, but it wouldn't be pretty.

When he opened his eyes, he knew he'd made a serious mistake bringing Victoria here.

The sun filtered around them on the sidewalk table, setting the perfect scene. The street was quiet and several birds settled into a tree beside them, offering a quiet serenade.

It should have been a romantic interlude for two people who were very much in love.

Instead, it was a quiet time for two adversaries to regroup and set their strategies. But Russ was beginning to suspect he'd made a tactical error. His concentration was not on the job ahead, but on Victoria.

Her obvious enjoyment of her double-decker ice-cream cone was causing him extreme discomfort. Her tongue curled around the cold confection, her face reflecting a sensual delight that made him squirm. He cleared his throat and she glanced up to smile at him.

''You know me awfully well after those few dates. I probably wouldn't have responded to any other bribe. Are you sure you don't want anything?'' Her tongue stretched out to catch a drip of ice cream.

''No.'' He swallowed. ''That cookie at Kelly's filled me up.'' He couldn't admit that watching her pure enjoyment was more than enough to satisfy him. He'd worry about food for the stomach later.

She leaned back and ran her tongue across

her lips. "My tongue's frozen. Want a lick?" Holding out the cone, she waited expectantly.

When he leaned forward, she pulled the treat away, a teasing gleam in her eyes. "Maybe I shouldn't share. You haven't been very nice to me today."

Russ folded his arms and leaned back in the wire chair, a touch of a smile on his lips. "I've been a perfect gentleman. On the other hand, you've been underhanded and deceitful."

"Me?"

He nodded.

She savored her treat and smiled.

Russ pulled at his shirt front. "You call this being nice?"

"Maybe I do owe you something. Not an apology of course. All's fair and all that. I didn't expect Kelly to go quite that far to stop you. Of course, the stain is actually Charles's fault, isn't it?" She took a small bite of her ice cream. "But I couldn't have possibly convinced him to do my dirty work for me. He's too young to understand that you men always stick together, no matter what the age."

She stretched across the table again and offered him the cone. "Bribery won't change my mind, Vicky."

"Don't call me Vicky. And I'm not bribing you. I'm simply sharing."

He wrapped his fingers around her wrist and held her hand still while he licked at the concoction. When she tried to pull away, he sunk his teeth into the ice cream and pulled away a huge chunk.

"Hey, no fair. I didn't say you could have it all." Her lower lip pushed out in a pout, forcing him to laugh.

"You're worse than a little kid."

"When it comes to my ice cream, you're right."

"I'll buy you another one if you're still hungry when you finish that." He'd buy her the entire ice-cream store just for the pleasure of watching her.

Her eyes gleamed greedily as she took her own bite. "Promise?"

"You'll get a bellyache."

"Let me worry about my stomach. You just worry about how you're going to pay for all of this." She crunched into the waffle cone.

He shifted in the chair, needing a change of subject, needing to get back to the reason he was chasing this woman all over the town of Jackson. "What's the plan for this afternoon, partner?"

Her eyes darted away from his intense stare. "*I* have an appointment. You must have physical therapy or something to go to. Or is it time for your nap?''

He knew she'd never give up trying to lose him, but he wasn't going to let it be this easy. ''I've cleared my calendar just to be with you. So who's *our* appointment with?''

''*My* appointment is with another informant. Kind of an informant.'' She chewed thoughtfully. ''Well, maybe just a person who can give a unique perspective on what's happening.''

Russ raised an eyebrow. ''Sounds interesting. Who is it?''

''Sometimes, you sound like a broken record.'' Victoria pondered the remaining tip of her cone. ''Her name is Madame Plotsky.''

Russ groaned and dropped his head back against the chair trying not to remember the last case he'd worked on that involved Madame Plotsky. ''I thought you were a logical person, one of those people who worked with cold, hard facts.''

''I am. But I'm also willing to utilize every possible avenue to get what I want. And Madame Plotsky has proved valuable in the past.''

''A fortune-teller has actually given you information that panned out?'' His voice reflected his disbelief.

She gulped, knowing she'd never admit that the most important piece of information had been about Russ himself. Just after her third date with Russ, Victoria had gone to the old woman to do a story on fortune-tellers and had gotten a private reading as part of her research.

The woman had warned Victoria about Russ, telling her that the man would change her life path. Madame Plotsky had outlined two very different lives for Victoria and had told her she had a choice between career or family, but that she couldn't have both without destroying herself. Victoria had canceled her next date with Russ, terrified of the implications of the reading.

She'd spent weeks trying to convince herself it was just a foolish conjecture from a con woman, but deep down inside, she'd known. Had always known. From the first moment she'd seen Russ she knew he was the one man who could make her think about changing her dreams.

''Victoria?''

His voice jerked her back to the present and she forced a smile. ''Her information has been . . . interesting. And it's pointed me in directions that have eventually paid off.''

She forced herself to look into his mirrored sunglasses while she told the tale. His silence made the lie seem to grow in proportion and she was certain he was onto her. She'd never been able to lie worth a darn, but this was such a little one.

He shifted, then grinned. ''Is that your polite way of telling me it's none of my business?''

Victoria muffled her sigh of relief and finished the last bite of her cone. ''If that's the way you choose to take it, who am I to argue with you?'' She stood, dusting the crumbs from her hands.

''So what time do we see her?''

''Russ!''

He took off his dark glasses and cocked his head to study her. ''Yes?''

''You're impossible.''

''So I've been told. What time?''

''I'm going to meet her alone. She'll sense your animosity and won't talk with me.'' Madame also might be tempted to say something that would give Victoria's feelings away, feelings she wasn't ready to acknowledge even to herself.

''I'll follow you either way, so you may as well make it easy on both of us and tell me.''

Her teeth came together with a snap as she struggled to hold onto her temper. She remembered Kelly's suggestion, but could think of no way to deter this particular elephant from his present course. Somehow, she'd just have to make the best of things.

"No wonder you were so successful as a cop. You just wore down everyone's resistance until they gave up out of sheer frustration."

His expression sobered and she immediately regretted her use of the past tense. Awkwardly, she reached out to touch his arm. "And you'll be even more proficient after this short vacation."

She turned away, expecting him to follow. But when she didn't hear his measured pace, she stopped. And her heart twisted in sympathy. He was still standing by the table, a haunted look in his eyes.

"I might not be able to go back."

The words were barely audible, but the pain behind them carried through the distance separating them and she couldn't stop herself from going to him.

Instinctively, she wrapped her arms around his broad chest and leaned her head against him. "It'll be all right, Russ. Somehow, there's a reason for all this. Maybe there's something better waiting down the road for you, a new path, a better career."

He shook his head, his arms still hanging limply at his sides. "My work is my life. I don't want to do anything else."

She looked up at him and watched as he stared blankly into a future that must be terrifying even to contemplate. Releasing him, she took his hand and gently tugged. "Come on. We'll be late. And Madame Plotsky is a stickler for promptness."

He followed her, but she wasn't certain he even knew it. Careful of his leg, she stuffed him into her small car and drove off, not knowing how to comfort such a deep pain.

But she did know one thing. His torment had touched her heart, nudging some unnamed emotion from her. And it scared her silly. Because all of a sudden she was vulnerable to his wounded spirit in spite of her best efforts to keep him at a distance.

She'd done her part, had paid the debt she owed him. But the urge to escape had been watered down by her exposure to Russ. Her thoughts went back to the night she'd canceled their date and told him she wouldn't have time to see him anymore. She'd thrown herself into her work, making sure she had little time to rethink her actions.

A few days later, a call had come over the police monitor about a hostage situation going down, and she'd responded with the newspaper's photographer. As usual, she had been in the middle of everything, trying to get her story.

When the first shots were fired by the suspect, she'd been caught in the open, a perfect target for a madman. Russ had knocked her to the ground and rolled behind a car with her clutched in his arms.

After allowing herself one comforting moment in his strong embrace, she'd pulled free, coolly thanked him, and walked away, more determined than ever not to let him into her life.

So she'd taken Kelly's challenge—she'd dragged him out of his despair, had given him a taste of life again. Wasn't that enough? Couldn't she just walk away again and consider the debt paid? Would he let her? She glanced over at his frozen features and hesitated. Against her better judgment, she wanted a little more time with him. Just one more afternoon wouldn't hurt. It was a brief enough moment out of her life.

She turned up the car radio, not ready to talk, to share too much with him just yet. His emotions were too close to the surface and she didn't want to take the chance of spilling out her own confusion over being this close to him. Either the tactic worked, or Russ was too wrapped up in his fear to say anything.

She didn't want to care about him. She didn't want to feel his anguish. But if he said much more, she would. And she'd have to try to help him, to fix the problem. It was a weakness of hers, this need to fix everyone she stumbled across. But it made for some wonderful stories in the feature section because she was able to get to the very heart of the story.

Stopping the car in front of a small, well-kept house, she turned to Russ. ''Are you coming inside?''

He seemed to pull himself back from a deep thought as he turned to look at her. The fear was still lurking there in the depths of his gray eyes, but he seemed to have it under control again. ''I know you won't tell me what happens, so I'll come hear it for myself.''

She saw one last chance to save the meeting and grabbed it. ''I'll tell you everything. Promise.'' Pulling a small tape recorder from her purse, she waved it in front of him. ''In fact, I'll record the whole thing. You can listen to it afterward.''

She grabbed for the door handle, anxious to escape before he could argue. ''You sit here and rest, get some sun, and I'll be back before you know it.''

She was congratulating herself on the clever escape as she rang the doorbell. But when Madame Plotsky opened the door, her eyes immediately fixed on a point behind Victoria. Knowing what she'd see, Victoria turned and saw Russ standing a few feet behind her, smiling.

''Nice try,'' he said.

She opened her mouth to protest, then snapped it shut again. Madame Plotsky would have enough to deal with without Victoria adding to the tension in the air.

''Come in, please.'' The older woman swept her hand toward the inside of the house, the oversized sleeve of her billowing white blouse floating around her arm.

Victoria tried to see the woman through Russ's eyes and almost made an excuse to come back later. The woman was an eccentric, pure and simple. Her gray hair was swept up in a elaborate coil while her jewel-framed glasses glittered in the sunlight. The long black skirt barely covered shiny gold slippers and the heavy scent of incense wafted outside to greet them.

Victoria dared one warning glance at Russ, then stepped inside.

''I see you've brought a guest.'' Madame Plotsky spoke with a heavily accented voice in a low, soothing tone that almost managed to quell Victoria's fears of Russ upsetting the meeting. Almost.

''A friend who has a vested interest in the outcome of the case I'm working on.''

Madame Plotsky fixed her gaze on Russ, her eyes becoming unfocused for a moment. Then, she nodded. "Yes, a very vested interest. Follow me. I will see what I can do to help."

They were seated in the living room on an overstuffed couch. Madame served tea, handing each of her visitors a china cup. Victoria almost laughed when Russ took his, sniffed it suspiciously, and curled his lip before setting it quietly aside. Victoria took a cautious sip, then put hers down to join Russ's. Whatever the brew was, it smelled terrible and tasted worse.

Madame first looked at Victoria. "I warned you, but you didn't listen."

Victoria squirmed, feeling like she'd been caught cheating in school. "It's only temporary. Until this case is resolved."

Madame raised an eyebrow that spoke volumes. Victoria wanted to argue with that eyebrow, but knew better. Besides, she knew that Madame knew exactly what was happening, knew that Victoria was desperate to stop her feelings without a clue as to how.

Victoria dared a glance at Russ, who was leaning back, staring at her intently. She had the disconcerting thought that he knew exactly what Madame was referring to. But he couldn't possibly have a clue as to what he had been predicted to do to her carefully structured life.

''Let me concentrate for a moment.'' Madame closed her eyes, breathing slowly and steadily. Suddenly, her eyelids snapped open and she fixed Russ with her sharp gaze. ''It all revolves around you.'' Madame Plotsky paused as if waiting for more information. ''Look to your past and you will see the clues you need.''

Russ frowned and shifted positions.

''Is this connected with a past case of his?''

Victoria wanted to demand names, dates, details, but knew she wouldn't get them. Madame only gave her clients enough information to nudge them in the right direction. She had always said she wasn't there to provide all the answers, just to guide and assist.

Madame smiled, the look managing to appear serene, yet eerie at the same time. ''He will know if he just concentrates on the past.''

Victoria wanted to howl in frustration. Another connection with Russ, another reason for her to stay close to him, to be exposed to the temptation he offered.

''Once you have settled the past, young man, you can move on to a new future, a new life. Resolve the old, make peace with it, and then move on. This next phase of your life will

bring unexpected pleasures and uncommon re-
wards. And it will satisfy a creative urge
you've suppressed for far too long.''

Russ sighed, the release of breath sounding
more like a snort of disgust.

Madame turned to Victoria. ''And you,
young lady, will be forced to finally make a
choice. You must choose between what you
think you want and what is truly going to make
you happy.''

Victoria turned the words over in her mind.
She thought she wanted Russ. So Madame
must be telling her to give up that desire, to
concentrate on her career like Victoria had always planned.

A strange loneliness nibbled at the edges of
her consciousness. That had always been the
plan—to concentrate on her career. But she
wanted more, wanted it all. She wanted love
and laughter, career and family. But she'd seen
firsthand what that life could do to a family, to
a woman. And she had vowed to never expose
anyone she cared deeply for to those dangers.

''Can you give us any more information? Is
there any one thing I should be concentrating
on?'' Victoria leaned forward, trying to keep
from looking at Russ.

''You will find the way. Just pay attention

to what has already gone before. The answers
will come from the past.''

Victoria thanked the woman, slipping her
two folded twenty-dollar bills on their way out.
She looked up to see Russ glaring at her and
darted out the door before he could embarrass
her.

''I can't believe you paid her for that hog-
wash.'' Russ chased after Victoria as she hurried down the sidewalk.

''She gave me good information. Now I
have something to look for.'' Victoria slipped
into the car, throwing a strand of hair behind
her shoulder.

''She gave you a line of fancy patter that
could mean anything. I just hope this can go
on your expense account, because you sure
wasted your money.''

Victoria bit her lip to keep the angry words
from flowing out. Russ was entitled to his beliefs. And she was entitled to hers. What she
needed now was time to think, time to mull
over the cryptic information and plan her next
move. And to do that, she had to get rid of
Russ.

She dropped him off at his car, almost hoping it wouldn't start and she could leave him
stranded for a while. But as usual, her luck was
against her and he pulled in behind her, staying

very close for the entire trip, almost as if he were afraid she'd try to ditch him.

Driving to the newsroom, she tried to make some sort of plan. She had to file two stories for tomorrow and wanted to write up some extra ones so she could be out in the field for a few more days. Her lips twitched into a smile as her plans fell into place. She'd bore him into leaving.

One thing she remembered plainly about Russ was that he had little patience for just sitting and waiting for something to happen. He'd once complained about a stakeout—endless hours of nothing with very few results. After an hour of watching her work, he'd be more than willing to leave her to her own resources. But she couldn't be too obvious about it.

When he pulled into the parking slot beside her, she rolled down her window. "I have some work to do in the office. Would you like me to meet you somewhere later?" She already knew the answer, but had to ask or he'd become suspicious.

"I'll go in with you. Maybe my past will jump up and bite me on the nose and I'll be able to solve this case before bedtime."

"It might be worth thinking about. You've handled a lot of cases over the years. Does one of them bear any resemblance to this one? Is there someone who's threatened to get even or threatened to kill you?''

''I lost count after the first hundred threats, Victoria. A cop learns not to dwell on that kind of thing.''

She got out and locked her car, trying not to think of the danger he'd faced on a daily basis. Taking a deep breath, she concentrated on making him want to leave. ''I need to powder my nose,'' she said sarcastically, ''then I'll be working at my desk. I'll meet you in the newsroom.''

When she came out of the bathroom, she ground her teeth together to hold back the anger. He was standing outside the door, leaning against the wall like he owned it. ''I think I'm safe here, officer. No need to stand guard.''

He took her elbow as he fell into step beside her. ''I just didn't want you running away again. I'm too old to go chasing after you all the time.''

She tried to ignore him, but his touch was igniting a small fire along the skin of her arm. She dragged a chair up beside her desk and motioned for him to sit, then proceeded to try to ignore him as she worked at the computer.

But he sat there, arms folded and feet

crossed at the ankles, watching her. Watched and waited like a cat getting ready to pounce.

He knew something.

Russ must have sensed something at Madame Plotsky's. And suddenly he was twice as dangerous. Because she could tell he was planning, plotting, and scheming. Without even being aware of his effect on her, he was planning on taking something from her she wasn't prepared to give up.

Her freedom and her future.

Chapter Six

The station had that hushed atmosphere that came over it just after the daytime staff left for the day. Trying to absorb some of that quietness, Russ leaned back in the hard chair, striving to appear nonchalant. But with Jayk staring at him, assessing him with that look only cops and schoolteachers had mastered, Russ was finding the charade almost impossible.

"Why do you want a listing of all your cases?"

"Just a hunch. You know, one of those crazy feelings that rarely pan out, but just might." Russ rested his ankle on his knee and waited, hoping his friend wouldn't ask.

"Why?"

Such a simple question. And if he answered it, Russ knew Jayk would think his friend had finally lost it—that the walls of the house had finally closed in and taken his sanity. He remained silent, feeling like a schoolboy in the principal's office.

"It's Victoria, isn't it?"

"Well, she gave me an idea."

Jayk sighed. "How could these robberies be related to any of your past cases? You've never covered jewelry store heists, have you?"

"No. Like I said, it's just a feeling."

"Spill it, bud. I'm not doing a thing until I know the entire story."

Russ pulled a hand across his face and knew he was cornered. "We went to see a psychic yesterday. Madame Plotsky."

Jayk groaned. "Not the one who calls us every time someone is reported missing?"

Russ managed a smile. "The same. Victoria's worked with her before."

"Why doesn't that surprise me?"

"The woman is a bit weird. But what she said made sense, hit me in that special place in my gut, made me think. I can't ignore that feeling, Jayk." He knew he was grasping at straws, but it was his only lead so far.

"But, what—?"

Russ leaned forward to interrupt. "Would you ignore it, Jayk?"

Jayk sighed and stroked his mustache. "No. I don't know of many cops who would. At least not the good ones." He pulled a clean sheet of paper out from under a stack of reports. "What was your starting date here?"

Russ gave his friend the information he needed, then stood to leave. "Thanks, bud. Call me when you get it and I'll take everything home to study it. Maybe something will make sense."

The phone rang and Jayk held up a hand to stop Russ's departure. Jayk listened for a minute, then looked at Russ. "I think I may have a solution standing right here. I'll call you back in a few minutes and let you know." Jayk hung up the phone and stared at Russ thoughtfully.

"I don't like that look, Jayk. Maybe it's time for me to leave." Russ settled his large hand on the doorknob, but stopped when Jayk cleared his throat.

"You've been wanting some time with the kids, right?"

Russ turned and grinned. "Let me guess. The baby-sitter canceled and I'm the closest victim."

Jayk looked a little embarrassed. "I

wouldn't normally ask, but Kelly's been looking forward to this for a long time. It's our sixth wedding anniversary and I hate to disappoint her.''

''Maybe it's just what I need. Between making myself crazy in that empty house and chasing Victoria, I think I'm losing my perspective on life. Those two hoodlums you call kids will put me back on the right track.''

Jayk looked relieved. ''If it were just Tammy, Jimmy could handle it, but I don't think he's ready for Charles yet.''

Russ laughed, realizing the sound was growing less rusty with each passing day. ''I'm not sure anyone's really ready for Charles, including the world at large. What time do you want me there?''

Jayk glanced at his watch and grimaced. ''Can you make it by eight o'clock?''

''I can, but will you?'' Russ turned to leave.

''By the way, that's a nice shirt you're wearing.''

''A gift from Charles this morning. Maybe I shouldn't bother to change before going back. Of course, I don't want him to think I like looking this way either. See you later.''

''I'll try to have your case list by morning.'' Jayk hesitated before continuing. ''If you should have the opportunity, I wouldn't object

if Victoria got really busy on something else.''
At Russ's bark of laughter, Jayk flushed.
''Something that would keep her out of our
hair for the next twenty years or so.''

''I have no objections, Jayk, but you'll have
to give me some clues. I'm having a hard
enough time just keeping up with her.''

Grinning, Russ waved and continued down
the hall. A night with the kids was just what
he needed. Somehow, their innocence, their
sense of silliness, always helped him set his
world to rights.

He loved kids, had always wanted an entire
flock to fill up his house. But first, he had to
find the perfect woman to share it all with. Un-
bidden, Victoria's image slipped into his
thoughts. He couldn't think of a more unsuit-
able prospect. And no woman would want him
until he was healed and back to work. If he
was that lucky.

The depression he'd staved off for the last
two days hovered closer and Russ found himself hurrying outside, hoping to outrun it. He'd
just remembered what it was like to live and
he didn't want to go back to the four walls of
his living room, no matter what it cost him.

He jumped in the car, ignoring his leg's protest, and gunned the motor. He had to keep
busy, had to keep moving, or the black cloud

would catch him. And he didn't know if he had the strength to break away from it again.

Russ drove past a toy store and stopped to pick something out for his little friends. One toy became two and he soon had more than he could carry. Kelly would be furious. She was always insisting he spoiled her children, but he couldn't help himself. He loved to watch their faces light up when he brought them something. And if he were honest with himself, he'd admit that he needed the distraction of picking out each toy.

Stopping for a quick burger, he ate in the car as he drove into the foothills. Kelly and Jayk had stayed on Jayk's family ranch, liking the peace and quiet of the surrounding area. Russ had often dreamed of a similar life, but that dream had been carefully tucked away after his injury, not to be viewed again until he was healed and ready to return to his job.

Russ juggled his packages as he knocked on the door and waited for an answer. In the past, he'd always just walked in, announcing himself with a loud bellow, but since the baby was born, he'd learned better. One session with a tired Kelly chewing him out for waking Charles had been enough of a lesson.

The door swung open and the kitchen light spilled out in warm greeting. Russ pushed away the twinge of jealousy at the fullness of Kelly's life before stepping inside. He let his gaze sweep over his ex-partner in admiration. ''You look fantastic, lady.''

She smiled and swirled around, letting the full skirt of her soft blue dress float around her legs. ''Thank you, kind sir. I feel fantastic. And I can't thank you enough for pinch-hitting at the last minute. I desperately need a break from baby food and alphabet books.''

Russ walked into the kitchen and deposited his treats on the table. ''You told me you loved staying home.''

''I do. I wouldn't trade it for anything in the world. But sometimes I need to remember I'm an adult. Too many hours of nursery rhymes can turn your brain to mush.''

''Isn't Jayk home yet?''

Kelly sighed. ''He had a last-minute something or other. I'm meeting him at the station.'' Determination glinted in her eyes. ''And he will be ready to go when I get there.''

''Uncle Russ!'' Tammy hurtled into the room, taking her usual flying leap into his arms.

Russ grunted, staggered backward, and feigned extreme pain. ''Young lady, you get a little bigger every day. Pretty soon, you'll be knocking me to the ground when you do that.''

Her laughter filled the dark corners of his heart. ''What'd you bring me?'' She wiggled, determined to see what was on the table.

Kelly gently tugged her daughter's hair. ''Wait a minute, missy. Kiss me good-bye first, then be a good hostess and offer Russ something to drink.''

Tammy dusted her lips across her mother's cheek, then jumped down to dart away. ''You can have water or pop, Uncle Russ. Now what did you bring me?''

Kelly rolled her eyes. ''Someday, she'll learn.''

Russ laughed. ''Maybe. In the meantime, I'll try to keep her out of trouble. Is Charles asleep?''

''For now. He's teething, so he may wake up cranky.'' Kelly stopped as she reached for the door. ''Are you sure about this, Russ? Charles can be a real bear and Tammy isn't always understanding when I can't give her my full attention.''

Russ nudged her toward the door. ''We'll work it out. Remember, I've been trained to handle large crowds and riots. Now, have fun and don't rush home. Uncle Russ has it covered.''

''Jimmy's with friends and should be home

in about an hour.'' She stepped outside in a rush of swirling silk and perfume.

The door closed with a click and he listened to Kelly's retreating footsteps. The slam of her car door coincided with the first cry of protest from Charles's crib. Tammy was busily digging through the packages on the table, discarding what was for her brother and making a stack for herself.

''Why don't you start a picture in that new coloring book? When Charles is quiet again, we'll make popcorn, okay?'' He fought his momentary attack of panic and forced himself to focus on one thing at a time.

''Yea, popcorn!''

But Charles had no intention of being quiet. He was hurting and he was mad about it and he was determined to let the world know. Russ rocked the baby like he'd seen Kelly do. He struggled to hold on to the squirming bundle when the baby really got mad and tried to put off Tammy's repeated demands for popcorn.

He had never felt so helpless in his entire life.

Thirty minutes later, when Victoria poked her head in the door, she expected to see total chaos. Instead, she found Russ doing the classic mother's dance of rocking back and forth from foot to foot while cuddling Charles in one arm.

Russ was softly singing a drinking song in his deep voice and Charles was listening intently. With his free hand, Russ was trying to tear open a package of microwave popcorn. Victoria quickly scanned the room for Tammy and found her busily building a small barn with a set of connecting building blocks. Crayons and puzzle pieces were scattered on the floor around her.

Victoria sighed with relief before entering the kitchen. If Russ had needed her to rescue him, they'd have both been in deep trouble. Her experience with children was very limited.

''Are you sure that's appropriate music for a baby to listen to?''

Russ spun around and dropped the popcorn bag. Charles started to cry the second the singing stopped and Tammy threw a handful of blocks across the room when they wouldn't do her bidding.

Victoria almost ducked out the door again. But she'd promised Kelly she'd look in on Russ and that was what she was going to do. Victoria had been an only child, had rarely baby-sat as a teenager, and was intimidated by anyone under the age of ten. But she'd promised. And Victoria Stephens never broke her promises.

Russ started singing again and bent to pick up the unopened bag of popcorn. When the bell on the microwave rang, he reached inside and pulled out a baby bottle, trying to test the temperature of the formula on his wrist. He glared at the spot of milk, shook some more out, then glared at the bottle.

With a frown of frustration, he handed the bottle to Victoria as he finished the last verse of the song. Then, in a singsong voice, he turned and spoke to her. "It's the only song he likes unless I'm talking to him and I ran out of things to say. I tried lullabies, but he only cries harder. Would you see if the formula is the right temperature so I can stop talking? Because I know he'll be happy as long as he's eating and then I can help Tammy with her project and get the popcorn made."

Russ launched into another verse, his cheeks actually showing a few twinges of pink over the words. When Victoria stifled a laugh, he began to hum instead.

Charles whimpered. Victoria quickly tested the milk and poked the bottle in the baby's mouth. Russ stopped humming with a sigh of relief. "That song is much more fun with a bunch of other guys in a bar." He tossed the bag into the microwave and set the timer, then walked over to Tammy.

''I want a tower over here and it won't go that way.'' She pushed her lips into a pout.

Russ settled Charles more securely in his arm and awkwardly hunched down to her level to study the barn. ''If you move this piece and go pick up those other ones, I think we can make it work.''

Tammy scampered across the room to do as he suggested, suddenly all smiles and obviously now pleased with her share of the attention.

Victoria watched in amazement. She'd expected to find the kids screaming and Russ in a total panic. But he seemed to have everything under control. In fact, he looked as if he were having the time of his life.

''You'd make a wonderful father.'' The words slipped from her mouth before she could stop them.

The joy washed from his face just before he turned away. ''Oh well, we can't always do what we're good at, can we?''

The timer rang and Victoria pulled a bowl from the cupboard. She emptied the popcorn into it, using the activity to buy herself a few seconds. This little domestic scene was confusing her, muddling her dreams and desires.

Russ had always had a habit of doing that and Victoria wanted to run.

But she'd promised Kelly. And she wanted to see what happened next. The temptation was too great to see how Russ would continue to handle the two children.

By the time the baby's bottle was empty, the popcorn had disappeared. Russ talked Victoria into reading Tammy a story while he tried to put an exhausted Charles to bed.

Victoria settled in the corner of the couch with the book Tammy had picked out. When the little girl curled trustingly into her side, Victoria almost sighed her pleasure. It felt so right, so perfect—like she'd finally come home.

By the second page, Victoria allowed her arm to creep around her new friend; by the third, she'd snuggled the girl into her lap. When the book was finished, she looked down to find Tammy sleeping in her arms. Victoria allowed herself to stroke the baby-soft hair and pressed a kiss on the top of her head.

''You'd make a wonderful mother.''

She glanced up, feeling a touch of guilt at being caught enjoying her role so much. Russ was lounging in the doorway and had obviously been watching her for some time.

''It's easy to love someone so small and

sweet. But I wouldn't want to make a full-time job of it.'' The words hurt, but Victoria had to say them, had to convince herself she didn't want children in her life.

His eyes reflecting his doubt at the truth of her words, he moved closer. ''Let me take her to bed.'' Russ reached down and took the sleeping girl into his arms.

Before straightening, he touched his lips to Victoria's, setting off a swamp of conflicting signals inside her. Without another word, Russ left the room and Victoria sat very still, trying to sort through the new feelings bombarding her.

She'd heard of a woman's biological clock ticking, of the urge for children growing stronger with age, but she'd never expected it to happen to her—had been *determined* it wouldn't happen to her. And it certainly wasn't supposed to explode inside her with such a flare of intensity. It was supposed to creep up slowly, give her time to get used to the idea or push it away. But right now, the idea of her own children was tempting—more than tempting.

She was twenty-eight years old, old enough to know what she wanted out of life—she wanted her career. Her own mother had worked a demanding job and tried to raise a child, but the child had always seemed to lose out when things got crazy.

Victoria could still remember her pain when a promised outing was canceled or when her mother had been too busy to talk. Her father hadn't been there for her either; being a busy man trying to survive in the hectic corporate world had left him little choice.

Her career was her life, her reason for being. And she had plans. Big plans for a future that left little room for anyone else in her life. A husband would be burden enough; a child would make it impossible. But Russ tempted her to give it all up. Victoria knew that would be a huge mistake. She also knew herself well enough to know that she'd eventually blame Russ for changing her dreams.

She needed to be strong, to force herself to remember her goals.

When Russ walked into the room, Victoria felt all her determination fade. He was smiling, his gray eyes glowing with soft satisfaction. ''I could get used to that.''

''What? Taking care of kids?'' She squirmed to the edge of the couch when he sat within a few inches of her.

''Yeah. I've always wanted kids, but I don't want to be one of those dads who just pats them on the head and gives them their allowance. I want to be actively involved in raising my kids.''

''You're a brave man. I don't think I could do it.'' His arm slipped across the back of the couch, close enough so that she could feel the heat from his skin, but not close enough to touch her.

She licked her lips nervously. Her body was screaming for him to touch her, but her mind kept insisting it would be a big mistake. Almost as big a mistake as when she'd gone to his house to appease Kelly and allowed him access to her life again.

''You don't want kids?''

''I've never had that urge. My career is enough to satisfy me.'' *Until now.* She stifled the thought, afraid Russ would sense her new confusion.

His finger traced a tantalizing path across her cheek and she almost sighed with pleasure. He was so gentle, so caring . . . so male.

And she wanted him.

There, she'd let the words come to the surface of her thoughts, had admitted to her feelings. There was no flash of lightning, no puff of green smoke, just the silence of the room. She wanted Russ in her life, wanted him to touch her, wanted him to be nearby.

Maybe now that she'd been honest with herself she could deal with the unwanted desires. Because she was smart enough to know she could never maintain a simple friendship with Russ.

"You're a natural with kids."

"That's not possible. Anyone under the age of ten might as well be from Mars, as far as I'm concerned."

"They don't know that. They trust you, sense something special about you." He edged closer, crowding her space, but she couldn't make the protest form on her lips.

"I saw the look on your face when you were holding Tammy. You want kids as much as I do. You just won't admit to it."

His finger smoothed across her bottom lip and she trembled deep inside. She'd already admitted to more than she was ready to deal with tonight. "I don't want children enough to give up my career. And I don't believe a woman can do both."

"That could be a problem."

Russ pulled away and Victoria bit her lip to keep from protesting. She'd apparently managed to turn him off by admitting she didn't want a family. Which was exactly what she'd wanted to accomplish. Once he realized there was no future with her, he'd back off, stick to the job at hand, and leave her alone. The thought left Victoria feeling very lonely.

Russ snapped off table lamp, plunging the room into a soft shade of darkness. He returned to her side and pulled her into his arms.

"Maybe I can find a way to change your mind about that career."

His lips brushed against hers and she closed her eyes, opening to him in a way she'd never allowed herself. He felt so right beside her; she felt so complete when he was around. Melting against his hard chest, she let his mouth tease her lips, savoring the taste and feel of him.

When he pulled back, she reached for him, tugged him closer, and kissed him, teasing his lips. His arms tightened and Victoria began to worry that she'd started something she had lost control over.

The creak of the screen door dragged them apart and they stared at each other for a long moment, both confused by the emotions raging through them. Russ stood and walked into the kitchen, leaving Victoria alone, confused, scared, and wanting.

"Hey, Jimmy. How's it going?"

Russ's voice boomed through the room, causing Victoria to wince. She'd allowed him to touch her heart and now she'd have to pay the price. Now she'd have to pull away and she'd be the one hurt. Because she was certain Russ would soon find someone or something else to amuse himself with. He wouldn't expend the effort to pursue her forever.

Russ was challenging Jimmy to a video game playoff. The lights came on without warning and Victoria fought the blush that threatened her cheeks when Jimmy grinned at her, his teenage mind certain of what he'd interrupted.

The sounds of warring spaceships filled the room, giving Victoria the chance to excuse herself. She stood in the kitchen and stared out into the silence of the night, wondering how her world had gotten so badly out of kilter in just a few short days.

Russ played the game with Jimmy halfheartedly while trying to listen to Victoria's movements. He hadn't meant to upset her, but he could tell he had. He just wasn't certain why. Was it the conversation about children? Or was it the fact that he'd kissed her?

Seeing her cuddling with Tammy had stirred something deep inside him, reminding him of why he'd asked Victoria out in the first place.

He'd been a rookie officer handling a difficult case. An eleven-year-old girl had been attacked by a stranger and Russ was the only officer available to interview her at the emergency room. But the girl had been too terrified to talk with him.

Finally, Russ had grabbed the nearest available female and enlisted her help. Victoria had been there following up on one of her stories and had reluctantly agreed to try.

The little girl had cried on Victoria's shoulder and Victoria had held her for almost an hour, talking softly, soothing, coaxing, until finally the story was told. He suspected he had fallen just a little bit in love with Victoria that day, but he'd never managed to break through her reserve again.

Until tonight.

And now that he'd been granted a little peek at what a future with Victoria held, he intended to pursue her. He had the perfect excuse for staying close. But he was confident he could parlay that into something deeper. When this case was over, he would have a relationship that was more than just friendship with Victoria Stephens.

She just didn't know it yet.

Chapter Seven

The shrill ring jerked him from a deep sleep, the first he'd managed in months. He groped for the telephone while struggling to hold on to the fading snatches of his dream. He'd been with Victoria, had just tunneled his fingers into her thick blond hair, and was pulling her closer until their lips were almost touching. Just another breath and—

"There's been another one."

He jerked to alertness, the dream disappearing like a popped balloon. "Where?"

"The Jewelry Mart." Victoria's voice was laced with suppressed excitement. "And the security guard was shot."

Russ struggled to fight off the sheet tangled

around his legs. He had to get dressed, had to get down there, had to see the evidence while it was still fresh. "I'll pick you up in ten minutes."

She hesitated and he prepared himself for an argument.

"I'm at the office." He could hear her draw in a ragged breath. "I'll be waiting out front."

He almost dropped the receiver at her easy agreement. "Make that five minutes, then." Scrambling to find his clothes, he pushed the receiver toward the cradle, hoping it would connect.

He'd been so exhausted last night, he'd simply dropped everything as he'd stumbled toward the bed. Picking up the carrot-stained shirt, he frowned at it, then wadded it up and tossed it in the corner. Grabbing a clean T-shirt from the closet, he jammed on his shoes while tugging the shirt over his head.

Keys. Where had he put the car keys? What little he'd had left of his mind had been concentrated on Victoria last night, not on paying attention to what his hands were doing. He made a quick tour of the house, finally spotting the keys on the floor by the front door. Whatever had possessed him to leave them there was a mystery never to be solved.

His leg protested as he tried to hurry down

the outside steps, but he ignored it. He couldn't give in to the pain now, not when he was so close to finding some answers. As he darted in and out of the morning traffic, his mind played with the evidence the police had so far. Evidence that basically amounted to nothing.

Victoria was waiting impatiently in front of the newspaper office, her gray slacks and jewel-toned blouse pressed against her slender body by a light wind. When Russ pulled to the curb, she jumped in the car before he had managed a full stop. "Go, go! We might miss something."

He took off, barely noticing how bossy she sounded. Her impatience matched his as he struggled with his dejection at not being directly involved in this case. The adrenaline pumping through his system brought back memories of being in the middle of the action, a place he desperately wanted to be again.

When they arrived at the Jewelry Mart, Victoria tumbled from the car. She darted forward for several steps, then stopped to wait for him. Together, they approached the police barrier.

Russ reached for his badge to flash at the officer and felt a fresh twinge of loss when he remembered he didn't have it. Officers on long-term medical leave were asked to turn in their identification until they came back to work.

Frustration dug at his insides as he tried to think of a way past the uniform standing guard. The man was new, so he didn't recognize Russ, and he was probably a greenhorn rookie who followed all the rules to the very letter. But Russ hadn't counted on the determination of the woman walking beside him.

"Hi. I'm Victoria Stephens with the *Daily News.*" She pulled out a press card and waved it in the officer's face. "I need to get through here and get some pictures for the front page." She pulled a small camera from her purse and held it in front of her expectantly.

"I'm sorry, ma'am. No one's allowed inside until the lab team is done."

"I totally understand that, but our deadline is in less than an hour. How about if I just stand on the other side of this tape and take a few pictures?"

The officer shifted and darted a glance around the parking lot. "Okay, but don't go any farther."

Victoria stepped under the tape, holding it out of the way for Russ to follow her. At the officer's questioning gaze, she smiled. "My apprentice."

The officer nodded.

Victoria made a big fuss out of getting just the right angle for the camera. Russ watched with a tolerant amusement, remembering similar tactics on one of his own cases. And he'd let her get away with it, just like this officer was doing. She looked so innocent, so unlike a scheming reporter. It was difficult to say no to Victoria Stephens.

"Oh, this just isn't going to work. I can't get the right lighting." She glanced at the officer and pointed to the edge of the building. "Can I just walk down there a little ways? I won't touch anything."

The officer hesitated, then agreed.

Russ chuckled as he followed her around the corner. "Do you even have any film in that camera?"

"Of course not. It doesn't even work. But it usually gets me where I need to go." She stopped and surveyed the broken window on the side of the store. "I guess this is it. Where do we start?"

Russ grinned. "Now, it's my turn. Follow my lead. Watch where you walk and don't touch anything. We're just looking; we don't want to mess up any evidence."

He pushed open the front door and walked inside like he had every reason to be there. When he saw one of the lab techs working in the corner, he went over. "Hey, George. What's going on?"

The man turned away from the fingerprint powder he was sweeping across every available surface. "I'm coming up with more prints than we'll ever be able to identify. It's like trying to sort out a room after a herd of pre-schoolers have touched everything." George adjusted his glasses, then glared at Russ. "Are you supposed to be in here?"

"Jayk called and told me to stop by. Just in case anything here was similar to my case."

George nodded. "Good plan. How's the leg?"

"Slowly getting better. Where have you already dusted? I don't want to get into any areas you haven't cleared yet."

George sighed and pointed to the other side of the room. "I've got that half done. And Tim has already vacuumed for cloth fibers or whatever, so I think we're pretty much done there. Not that it will do us any good, but we're getting desperate enough to try anything."

"Who's doing the interviews?"

"Jacobson has the lot of them down at the station now. And Simms is waiting at the hospital for the security guard to come out of anesthesia. I hope the old guy saw something, because he's the best lead we've got right now.''

Russ dropped a friendly hand on George's shoulder. ''No one wants them more than I do. Keep at it and I'll let you know if I find anything you missed.''

He started to walk away but Victoria tugged at his hand. Her whisper was just loud enough to reach his ears.

''What good is it going to do us to look where they've already been?''

''I'm not going to take a chance of destroying the one piece of evidence they haven't found yet. We can't afford to contaminate the scene. But maybe, if we've lived right and are real lucky, we'll find something they missed in their sweep. I just want to get a feel for it and see what happened.''

Victoria glanced over her shoulder, her frustration evident. ''Okay, you're the boss on this one. But I'd really like to get a look in that safe.''

''Patience, Vicky. I'll get you in there later.'' He pulled her hand into his, liking the feel of her skin against his, but needing more to keep track of her right now. He was learning a lot about Victoria, and he was more attracted to her every day, but he still didn't completely trust her. Her story would always come first.

He began walking around the display cases, his shoes crunching across the broken glass. "Someone didn't waste any time. How long do you think it took them to clean all this out?"

"They don't usually leave much in these cases at night, do they? Why break all that glass for nothing?"

Russ stopped to think about her words. Why indeed? "None of the other crime scenes were this torn up. In fact, they were overly tidy, making the lab guy's job almost impossible." His eyes narrowed. "Maybe they wanted to make us look for something in the wrong places?" He turned and slowly surveyed the room with narrowed eyes. "Look." He pointed to the opposite corner.

"There's no damage there." She grinned. "And the lab has been through that corner, right?"

"Yeah, but not with the same perspective we're going to give it. Come on." A tingle of awareness traced down his spine.

Russ stuffed his hands in his pockets and just looked. Victoria reached out to touch one counter, but he grabbed her hand. "Trust me, you don't want to get that fingerprint powder on you. It's nasty stuff."

She nodded in agreement, but her blue-eyed

gaze was darting around like a hummingbird in flight.

Russ dropped to his knees and looked under the display case.

"What are you looking for?"

"I don't know. Something is bugging me, calling to me. One of those gut hunches we cops learn to listen to." His fingers probed the edge of the carpet. He moved down the wall, poking and pulling. When he came up with nothing, he sat on the floor and simply looked around.

"Tell me what to look for, Russ. I want to help."

"Shh." His eyes narrowed and he continued to study the corner. The door to one display case was cracked open a few inches. He leaned toward it, then scooted closer. Gently, he eased the door open and looked inside. "Yes!"

His whisper mirrored his triumph as he tugged and pulled until something broke free from the track of the sliding door. He carefully held up a heavy gold ring for Victoria's inspection.

"Isn't that just another ring from the display?"

"According to the note on the case, this is supposed to be all silver jewelry. And it looks like it was all taken out by the staff before the robbery. Besides, the ring is old. Look at the wear marks.''

He turned it over and felt his blood freeze in his veins. Memories swamped his thoughts, dragging him back to a dark alley, a black night, and endless agony. Sucking in a deep breath of air, he closed his eyes, trying to still the sickening thud of his heart.

''Russ? What is it? What's wrong?'' Victoria put her hand on his shoulder and shook him gently. ''Russ?''

''It's the same ring.'' His words seemed to come from a distant tunnel.

''What ring? What's going on? Tell me, Russ.''

''The guy who shot me was wearing this ring.'' The metal was cold in his hand, as cold as the man who had looked Russ in the eye and smiled just before pulling the trigger.

''How do you know that?''

His fingers curled around his find and he tried to distance himself from the scenes playing over and over in his mind. The pain, the blood, the disbelief. . . . ''When someone points a gun at you, your entire focus automatically goes to that weapon. That's why you always hear stories from witnesses of how big the gun was. It even happens to cops. When I was staring down the barrel of that gun, the streetlight reflected off his ring.'' His breath came out in a loud rush. ''I'll never forget that ring. And this is it.''

''May I see it?'' When Russ silently handed it to her, she pulled her hand back. ''Shouldn't we be careful of fingerprints?''

Russ shook his head. ''It's too ornate. Nothing would show up.''

Almost reluctantly, she took it. Frowning, she twisted and turned the gold band. ''It's certainly an ugly thing.''

Russ gave a bark of harsh laughter. ''It's even uglier wrapped around the grip of a gun.''

''There's an inscription. Initials. See?''

Russ snatched the ring from her hand and frowned at the barely visible engraving. A small glimmer of triumph crept through the shadows of the past. ''Good job, Vicky.'' He wrapped one hand around the back of her neck and pulled her closer. Pressing a hard kiss on her lips, he struggled to stand.

''The name is Victoria,'' she whispered as she pressed her fingers to her lips.

Russ felt a rush of satisfaction. He was getting to her—he was wearing her down. Before this was over, he'd have a chance to date her again. He wanted that, needed it. Because he'd always had the nagging feeling that he'd missed out on something special when she'd canceled their last date. And he wanted another chance to prove it.

"What are you two doing in here?" Jayk's cold voice cut through Russ's thoughts.

"Helping out."

"Russ, you know better—"

Russ held up his hand to stop the words, handing the ring to Jayk. "This was worn by the guy who shot me, Jayk."

Jayk took the ring and rolled it over and over, examining it carefully.

"Do you have that case list yet? I want to run a check on the initials inside. Maybe it matches up with something."

"That would be too easy." Jayk glared at Victoria, obviously wanting to reprimand her for being inside a crime scene, but he was too distracted by the value of Russ's evidence. "The lab guys missed this?"

"I doubt they realized what they were looking at. I did."

Jayk held the gold band up to the light, squinting at the inside. "You're sure about this? It could just be from another display. Maybe it was dropped there while they were trying to get something else."

"It's engraved on my memory for all eternity, Jayk. Find the owner of that ring and we've got our man."

Jayk handed the ring back to Russ. ''Turn it over to George and sign it into the chain of evidence. I don't want any loopholes for this guy to slip through once we catch him.''

Russ followed through with the paperwork, always aware of Victoria quietly hovering in the background. She watched everything intently and he could see her reporter's mind filing it all away for future use.

There was a brief twinge of regret that she wasn't just interested because it involved him, but he pushed it aside. When the case was resolved, then he would worry about a relationship with her. For now, his total focus needed to be on putting the man who shot him behind steel bars for a very long time.

''We make a good team.'' She followed him outside into the bright sunlight. ''Maybe we should start our own detective agency.''

The sunlight caressed his face and he turned toward the warmth, desperately trying to wipe away the dark memories. His sense of humor struggled to the surface and he was able to answer her. ''We could call it Stumble and Fumble. You find 'em, I'll fall on 'em.''

Scenes from that fateful night still crowded his thoughts and he desperately tried to shove them aside. Her laughter coaxed him closer to her, to her vitality, to her energy.

''That's terrible.'' Victoria stifled another giggle.

Russ studied her, trying to gauge her intentions. He wanted to spend more time with her. He wanted to get beneath that reporter's veneer and find the woman. But she'd always held back, always kept her job between them. Was that all she wanted—a business relationship?

As he remembered her response to him last night, a confidence he hadn't felt in months slowly seeped through him. If she thought she was going to get away with keeping him only as a friend, he'd simply have to change her mind.

He'd finally decided. He wanted Victoria in his life, wanted her close to him. For how long, he couldn't tell yet, but he needed the opportunity to test the waters and see where it would take them.

''I think this calls for a celebration.'' She grabbed his arm and tugged him under the taped barrier. The young officer standing guard frowned at them, but was distracted by another reporter just coming onto the scene.

''We haven't solved the case yet.'' He had to argue with her, couldn't let on that he'd do anything to spend some time with Victoria, the woman, without work interfering. She'd run like a scared rabbit if she suspected his thoughts.

''No, but we've made a major breakthrough. One thing I've learned in life is to celebrate every small victory. There are too many times when the final goal is simply too far away to do more than visualize it.''

''There have been days when I could relate to that.'' Her enthusiasm was contagious. ''Okay, where do we celebrate?''

''My house. We'll stop and pick up the fixings for a steak dinner. Give me a few hours to get my stories filed, then we can kick off our shoes and relax.'' The excitement shone in her blue eyes and Russ couldn't have denied her anything.

Victoria ran into the grocery store. Russ had volunteered to get dessert, and he walked over to a small French pastry shop. He played the events of the morning over in his mind and felt a deep satisfaction. After keeping her distance, after holding him at bay for all these months, he'd finally managed to break through her reserve. Now, he just needed to convince her that they had a chance of building something special together.

Russ clutched the cardboard bakery box. He needed Victoria, as well as wanted her. Just to survive, he needed her energy, her fight, her drive. But what did he have to offer her in return?

His free hand clenched in frustration. One more week and he'd have the answers.

One more week and the doctor would do a final evaluation on his leg.

One more week and his entire life would be decided with a few strokes of the doctor's pen.

''Will that be all, sir?''

The clerk's voice jerked Russ from his thoughts. He set the box on the counter and paid for it without paying the slightest bit of attention to what was happening.

One more week. Did he have the right to pursue Victoria? Did he want to stop?

He spotted her across the parking lot, her arms full of grocery bags, her hair swept by the wind, her eyes sparkling with life. He had to concentrate on the case first. Then, he'd worry about his future with this tantalizing woman. And any chance of sharing their to-morrows.

As they started toward each other, Victoria watched Russ carefully. She knew she was playing a dangerous game, knew she would re-gret letting Russ get this close. But she'd been lonely these last few months and he'd unex-pectedly filled that void in her life.

If she let him close for just a few weeks,

maybe it would be enough to stave off the haunting quiet of her apartment. This mood would pass, just like it always did, and then she'd get back to pouring all her energies into her job.

But her lips betrayed her as they began to tingle with the memory of his quick kiss this morning. And last night, he'd been so tender, so caring. She was tired of fighting the world alone, tired of pouring out her troubles to a stray cat who visited on the odd occasion when he was hungry.

Maybe it was time to take some of her savings and invest in a house of her own. Then she could have a dog, maybe several pets. That should be enough. When this investigation was over, she'd break off with Russ again and do some house hunting.

It was time for her to settle down, to get away from the gypsy life of an apartment dweller. In the meantime, she had every intention of enjoying Russ's company for a while. After all, he'd already warned her that she wouldn't be able to get rid of him. So, why fight the inevitable?

"That looks like a lot of groceries for the two of us." Russ stopped beside the car and peaked into the tops of the sacks.

"I thought as long as I was in there, I might as well get a few other things."

She didn't mention that those things included candles for the table, a small spray of flowers, and some new cloth napkins. It wasn't that she was trying to dress things up for Russ, she just needed to indulge herself a little. She'd been working hard lately, maybe too hard. A little treat now and then was a necessity.

She sighed as Russ unlocked the car door. She was struggling to justify being with Russ and she shouldn't have to do that. Why couldn't she just enjoy their time and forget about tomorrow?

Madame Plotsky's voice came back to haunt Victoria, the tone and the words a warning of change that she couldn't accept in her life. Couldn't there be a compromise, a middle ground?

They stopped at the police station next and Russ picked up his case list. Victoria was dying to see it, but was willing to let Russ have the first look. It would mean more to him than her anyway. Once they arrived at her office, Russ sat quietly at the side of her desk and paged through the lengthy list while she tried to concentrate on her work.

Victoria found herself hurrying through her assignments, for once anxious to leave early.

Normally, she hung around until the last possible moment, always afraid she'd miss something or lose a chance to take on that next big story.

Tonight, someone else could have the stories. She wanted to be with Russ.

''Find anything?'' she asked as she shut down the computer for the night.

Russ was glaring at the papers as if they'd offended him. ''No. Not a single thing.'' Dragging his fingers through his shaggy brown hair, he sighed. ''Nothing here comes close and none of the people I've arrested match the initials on that ring.'' He glared at the ceiling. ''I hate to put too much stock in Madame Plotsky's words, but I was hoping she'd be right. I was counting on it.''

Victoria wanted to soothe his pain, to hold him close and offer comfort, but she was afraid to try. He was becoming important to her and if she wasn't careful she'd lose everything she'd worked so hard for. Not even Russ was worth that. ''May I look at it later? Maybe a fresh perspective would help.''

''It wouldn't hurt.'' His fist thumped against her desk. ''I was so sure. Or maybe I was just desperate. It would have been too easy this way.''

Russ brooded during the drive to Victoria's

apartment. She let him have his silence, trying not to let herself care too much. But that was becoming impossible. Madame Plotsky had been right. Russ would destroy Victoria's chosen way of life. But suddenly the years ahead loomed long and empty, something that had never happened before.

Would she regret her single-minded determination when she was forty? Fifty? Would she still be chasing the elusive excitement of the siren or be chained behind a desk? Would she still be around at sixty or would she have faded away from sheer loneliness by then?

When they entered her small apartment, Victoria looked around, took note of how barren the room looked, how lacking it was in shared warmth. She'd struggled to decorate it on a very limited budget, but it was too much a woman's room, too neat, too sterile. It needed a man's clutter to bring it alive, to add that touch of feeling lived in.

She began to prepare the light dinner while Russ poured each of them a glass of iced tea. He sipped at his while he watched her. His eyes had a distant look, a faraway glaze that let her know he wasn't even in the room with her.

When he started massaging his leg, she knew he was reliving that night, turning it over and over in his thoughts to try to find the missing puzzle piece. But he'd only manage to drive himself crazy if he kept at it with this intensity.

''Would you make the salad?'' She didn't know if he was competent in the kitchen, but surely even he couldn't destroy a simple salad.

He jerked away from the door frame where he'd been leaning. ''I'm sorry. I got caught up in the case again. I'm not usually such a thoughtless jerk.''

He grabbed the head of lettuce and began shredding the leaves. Victoria watched his strong hands do their work, trying not to think about what those hands could do to her. She'd felt his touch, knew how gentle he was, how his strength sent sparks sizzling across her skin.

Lifting her glass to hide the flush covering her cheeks, she took a swallow of tea. But the tingling trail it left in her throat only reminded her of Russ's kisses—kisses that she wanted more of.

This entire evening had been a big mistake.

''Do you have a city map?'' He grabbed the mushrooms she'd purchased and started washing them.

''Of course. A reporter wouldn't be without one. Why?''

"You'll think I'm nuts."

"So what else is new?" She'd never admit that she was even crazier for playing with the fire he offered her.

"Low blow, lady." He chuckled. "But you may be right. Anyway, I was watching this cartoon the other day."

"Donald Duck or Bugs Bunny?"

"Neither. And I'll never tell which one." He pulled open drawers until he found a knife, then set out to demolish the mushrooms. "The bad guy was doing a string of robberies in a specific pattern as a message to the superhero, who of course immediately caught on and was waiting for the guy the next time he hit."

Russ managed a laugh. "I've tried a psychic; why not that? It'll give me something else to think about besides the possibility of failure."

Victoria put down the fork she'd used to test the baked potatoes and went over to him. She rested her hand on his arm until he stopped chopping and looked at her.

"You can't possible be a failure, Russ. You have too much going for you."

"Yeah, like a bum leg and no job."

"Stop it. Stop feeling sorry for yourself. People have got it worse than you and they're still happy and productive. They find a second career and get on with their lives.''

She shook the solid strength of his arm to be certain he was paying attention. ''There's another job for you. I'll bet if you allowed yourself to think about it, there's something else you'd really like to do with your life.'' She was surprised at the guilt her comment brought to his expression. ''What, Russ? What else do you want to do?''

He ducked his head a little. ''It's just one of those things that's crossed my mind a few times.''

One of those things he wasn't ready to talk about, Victoria decided quickly. Her fingers dug into the taut strength of his muscles. ''Let's get through this case, then we'll worry about what comes next, okay?''

His gray eyes watched her thoughtfully and she resisted the urge to squirm. She'd just hinted at a future for them even if it was only short-term. And suddenly she knew it was the best promise she'd ever made. The only promise she *could* have made.

Somehow, they'd work it out. Somehow, they'd find a way for both of them to be happy.

It would just take time, a lot of talking, and a bushel full of luck. Victoria felt a shudder of fear race through her. She'd never been big on luck. In fact she'd always felt she'd gotten the short end of the deal in that department. But she had to try, had to risk her heart and her future on this man.

Chapter Eight

"Well, that's a bust."

Russ threw the red marker down in disgust. Victoria carefully set the tray holding two cups of coffee beside the map and laughed softly at his frustration. "You didn't really expect it to work, did you?"

His mouth twisted into a grin. "No, but I'm ready to grab at anything."

"Don't rush it. Things will happen in their own time, just the way they're meant to."

"Now you're starting to sound like that Madame Plotsky." Russ stirred a spoonful of sugar into his coffee. "Things don't always work out. All too often, we have to push and

135

shove them in the right direction. You know that as well as I do.''

The urge to kiss him had been building ever since they walked in the door. Now it evaporated in a puff of irritation. Victoria tried to keep from bristling at his words, but the habit was too deeply ingrained. ''At least she keeps a positive attitude. She doesn't just give up and resort to pouting like some people do.''

''I don't pout.'' He slammed the spoon down onto the tray to emphasize his words.

''Right.'' She plucked up her spoon and dipped it into the sugar bowl. ''Have some more sugar. You need to sweeten your disposition.'' Dropping a hefty dose of sweetener into his cup, she glared at him in challenge.

He glared back.

When something in his eyes shifted, she realized her mistake. It was like teasing a hungry lion with a piece of meat. Russ had been looking for a fight since the day she'd walked into his house.

And she kept giving him one.

''You never quit. You just don't have the sense to give up, do you?'' His words were low, his tone dangerous.

Victoria tilted her chin upward, determined not to let him intimidate her. But inside, she was struggling to hold her ground. He was too powerful, too potent, too dangerous. ''I should be smart enough to give up on you because you certainly don't want to be saved from yourself.''

''You make me sound like a hopeless drunk living on the street.''

He *was* hopeless, but not in the way he was thinking. ''Well, you are drowning your sorrows, but you choose to use self-pity instead of booze.''

The anger drained from his eyes, to be replaced by something much more dangerous. His hand snaked out and curled around the back of her neck. ''Maybe you can suggest something better to drown myself in.''

She resisted, but he pulled her closer, slowly, teasingly. The promise of the touch of his lips tantalized her and, having kissed him before, she wanted to again. She wanted to be close to him, to know that he wanted her too. But not like this, not in anger. She tried to pull away, but her effort was halfhearted at best.

Victoria watched his mouth draw nearer, knowing she shouldn't allow him to kiss her. She resisted the urge to close her eyes, to block out the tempting sight of his mouth, forcing herself to watch him, afraid he'd pull some trick if she didn't. Some devious, underhanded thing like making her want him even more than she already did.

When they were less than an inch apart, his lips curved into a smile that matched the threat in his eyes. "Scared?"

She shook her head, determined to play out his bluff and to be the winner in their contest of wills.

"No, you wouldn't be scared of a mere man, would you Victoria?" His voice dropped to a low growl that sent a shiver racing through her. "You scare me, did you know that?"

Again, she shook her head, any possible answers clogging her throat.

"The more time I spend with you, the greedier I get. That scares me. I know you don't want me in your life, but I'm not certain I can simply walk away anymore. That scares me even more."

His lips brushed against hers and she had to force herself not to lean into him, to kiss him back. His words made her heart soar with hope, made her think anything was possible—until the reality of her life and her dreams intruded.

"Tell me I can stay around when the case is over. Tell me I can call you and ask for a real date." His lips refused to say the word, but his eyes added the "please."

She gulped as the web he was weaving

around her tightened. She wanted to fight, to pull away, but pride made her stay put. ''I can't.''

The words almost didn't make it past the lump in her throat. She wanted to tell him yes, that she wanted to share some time with him, but he threatened everything she'd worked so hard for. And she couldn't allow that to happen.

Before dinner, she'd weakened, had almost allowed him into her life. But now, with him this close, with the strength of the feelings flowing through her, she knew any time beyond the duration of the case would be a huge mistake.

This time, Russ shook his head. ''Not can't. You won't, Victoria. There's a big difference.'' His reluctance obvious, he drew his hand away from her neck and leaned back into the couch. His chest rose and fell as he sucked a deep breath into his lungs. She waited for his next move and was surprised when there wasn't one.

He reached for his coffee, took a large gulp, and grimaced. ''Even I don't need that much sweetness.''

Putting it back on the table, he shoved the map toward her, the slight tremor in his hand giving her a crumb of comfort. At least he was as affected by her as she was by him.

"Do you see anything there that I've missed?"

A beat of silence passed between them, a moment in time when their gazes touched and held, each asking for something the other couldn't give. She forced herself to look at the map, forced herself to concentrate on the red lines he'd drawn in several different directions. It looked like a child had tried to play connect the dots without knowing how to count.

The touch of his mouth on hers still lingered and she finally pulled her bottom lip between her teeth in a vain attempt to distract herself from the sensation, regretting the need to return to business.

"No, there's certainly no sign of a pattern there." Her finger tapped against the paper as she ordered her thoughts to concentrate on the job at hand, but the memory of his touch lingered in the background, taunting her. "Let's mark in the stores that haven't been hit. Maybe that will mean something."

Russ shrugged. "It couldn't hurt. Where's your phone book?"

She went and got it, relieved to escape the potent essence of Russ Connor. Even the insignificant length of her small living room made a difference. Calling off each address to him, she watched as his strong hands marked in the new locations. When they were done, they both stared at the map, needing to see something, anything, that would give them a hint.

Victoria stared until her vision blurred. With a slight shake of her head, she looked again. That was when she saw it. She reached out to grab Russ's arm, almost too excited to notice the sensations tingling over her skin at the touch. ''Russ. Look.''

He frowned. ''There's nothing there, Victoria. It was just another stupid idea.''

''No, it wasn't. Look again.'' Her finger began to point to several marks. ''It's every other one. He's hit every other jewelry store in the area.'' She tapped the last mark. ''And this one is next.''

Russ leaned forward, the excitement vibrating through him transmitting itself to her. ''You're right! I knew I could count on you.''

He fell silent and his excitement faded. When he turned to look at her with narrowed eyes, a cold finger of foreboding traced its way up her spine. The cold determination was back, along with the anger that drove him to keep at this.

''I'm not going to turn this over to the police. I want this arrest, Victoria. I don't want to share it with anyone.''

''Russ, you can't just go barging in there alone!'' She couldn't bear the thought of him being in that kind of danger, didn't even want to think of what could happen to him.

He held up a hand to silence her protests. ''I know it's stupid, it goes against all my training, but you of all people should understand. If I turn this over to Jayk, I'll be shut out. Since I'm on medical leave, I won't even be able to tag along. And I need to get my hands on the jerk who did this to me. I need to look him in the eye and ask him why.''

Russ fell silent, struggling with some inner demon. Victoria resisted the urge to reach out to him, to share his pain. It would bring them too close.

''It wasn't just a wild shot to slow me down. He wasn't even trying to kill me. When he saw me, he smiled and wasted precious seconds to take a deliberate aim at my leg, as if he had a score to settle.''

She shuddered at the image he was painting. ''You never told me this before.''

''I've never told anyone. It wasn't just a bad shot. This guy wanted to hurt me, to give me the kind of pain that went deeper than the physical. He was punishing me for a long, long time and he knew it.''

Russ scrubbed a hand across his face. ''That's why Madame Plotsky's words made so much sense, why I was so eager to believe her. But for the life of me, I can't figure out who would hate me that much.''

''Russ, I'm sorry.'' His words were shattering her, tearing her insides out.

She wanted to comfort him. She wanted to hold him and assure him it would be all right. But now, she wasn't sure anything would be right again. Not only was Russ's career possibly over, but she could be setting him up for another hurt. She didn't want him to care for her, but it felt so wonderful, she couldn't resist letting him.

''Did you know that if that bullet had been just a few inches lower, it would have shattered my knee? I would have been lucky to ever use that leg again if that had happened. As it is, I'm still marking a fine line.''

She knew it was the ultimate stupidity, but she suspected she'd done worse things in the name of her job. And this was to help Russ. The newspaper story wasn't even important any more. ''What can I do to help?''

He looked up, his disbelief reflected in his gray eyes. ''You won't snitch me off?''

''I should, but I won't. So how can we set this up with just the two of us and still keep you out of danger?''

A grin flooded his face and he winked at her. ''I think I love you, lady.'' He stared at the map for a minute, then began to outline his plans.

But Victoria wasn't listening. She'd gotten stuck on his line about love. It was just a joke, one of those things said in the heat of the moment. He didn't really mean it.

But suddenly, she wanted him to mean it.

And suddenly, she knew she was in even worse trouble than she'd ever imagined.

His plans washed over her as she struggled with an emotion so deep, so intense that she knew it would eventually break her heart.

And her dreams.

The sound of the doorbell echoed through the silent house. Victoria stood on the doorstep, tapping her foot. Madame Plotsky normally only saw people by appointment, so Victoria hoped she wasn't interrupting anything.

Victoria needed to see the woman and ask some specific questions—once she figured out what those questions were. She suddenly wanted to experience everything life had to offer—career, marriage, family, and whatever else came along.

But both the past and Madame Plotsky's words stood in her way. Victoria wanted to know if there was another way. She didn't want to make a choice. She wanted it all.

Footsteps approached the closed door. Madame opened the door with that serene smile that held the secrets of the world. "I've been expecting you. Please come in."

"I'm sorry I came without an appointment. I'll try not to take up too much of your time. I just have a few questions."

Madame stopped and studied Victoria. "I knew you would come sometime today and I've been waiting for you. We will find a way, so please don't concern yourself."

Madame sat in a flowered chair and poured two cups of tea. Victoria took her cup and set it on the table, remembering how awful the brew tasted the last time she'd visited.

"Drink," Madame ordered. "It will help clarify your thoughts." Her eyes twinkled with a brief touch of devilment. "It will taste better than the last time."

Victoria laughed as she remembered Russ's distaste. "You did that on purpose. You deliberately served Russ something awful."

"He was expecting bat's wings and lizard

tails. I was just doing my part to fulfill those expectations.''

Victoria sipped the tea, recognizing the taste of peppermint and something else she couldn't define. But the hot drink stopped her thoughts from chasing themselves around her head and she was finally able to form the questions she needed to ask.

''When I was here several years ago, you told me I had to choose between career and love.'' Victoria twisted her fingers together, then forced herself to take another sip of tea. Calm flowed through her veins. ''I want them both, Madame. There has to be a way I can do it without hurting anyone. I don't want my children to have the kind of family I grew up in, but I don't want to give up my career.''

Madame smiled. ''The last time you visited me, you were very set on your path. Since then, you have opened up to the possibilities and there are many more choices available to you.''

She reached forward and pulled Victoria's hand into hers. ''Trust in the future and be brave. You can have it all if you have the courage to grab it. And no one will be harmed by your needs.'' Her fingers squeezed gently. ''You have enough love, enough drive, to have it all.''

''But—''

''Trust, Victoria. It will happen the way it is meant to happen. And if you allow that, you will realize a happiness you never thought possible. Quit fighting for once and see what life has to offer.''

It sounded so simple.

As she was ushered out the door, Victoria couldn't help but compare Madame's words to what she'd told Russ the night before. He wasn't accepting the idea of blind trust in a nebulous fate any more readily than she was.

She hesitated before getting into her car. It was time to make some decisions, decisions that would set the course of her life, that could leave her satisfied with her choices, or forever nagged with the possibility she'd missed out on something wonderful.

Russ had wanted to meet for dinner to outline a plan of attack for tonight when they staked out the jewelry store at the mall. She was eager to see him, anxious to spend time with him. But she knew she was playing with fire.

Victoria twisted the key in the ignition with a smile on her lips that bordered on grim. She'd tease the lion and see what happened. Madame had indicated Victoria could have it all.

That was exactly what she wanted. Everything, right where she could touch it and savor it every day of her life.

She had the courage. Now she just had to see if Russ was man enough to accept her dreams.

With the fear temporarily washed away by Madame's words, Victoria could finally admit that she loved Russ. Yes, she loved him and wanted to spend her life getting to know him, sharing their lives and their laughter. She was being given a second chance with him and was determined not to run away this time.

Glancing at her watch, she noticed she'd be early for her meeting at the restaurant. That was okay, because she still needed some time to think. Now that the decision was almost made, she needed time to savor it, to dream of the possibilities offered to her so unexpectedly.

Ordering a cup of flavored cappuccino, Victoria stirred it slowly, watching the cream swirl into the dash of cinnamon on top. As she watched, fanciful ideas began to form in her head—ideas that she'd never allowed before.

Like the blend of spice and cream, her life could be that perfect mixture that would make it rich and flavorful. Without one aspect, there could not be the enjoyment of the other. If she had Russ to share things with, her work would become more meaningful, just as her work would enhance her relationship with a very special man. But any one thing taken by itself would lack the same wonder, because everything in life was better when it was shared.

When she looked up and saw Russ crossing the room, she knew she was right. Sharing this case with him had made it less important in the general scheme of her life. Before, the story had been everything, had taken her entire focus. But now, the story was blended with her relationship with Russ and it was more exciting, more consuming.

In the end, it would be a better, stronger story because of the new perspectives and insights she'd reached. Her writing in the past had been one-sided—one point of view. Now it would blossom with new depth. And so would her heart.

''Well, partner. Are you ready to go to work?'' Russ slipped into the chair across from her. He eyed her coffee with interest and finally reached across the table and picked up the cup. There was a certain intimacy in his actions that sent an unaccustomed warmth flooding through Victoria. But she couldn't stop her grin when he made a face at her drink of choice and carefully set the cup back in front of her.

The waitress stepped up to the table. "Would you care for a cappuccino too, sir?"

Russ shuddered. "I'll take some real coffee, preferably several days old and strong enough to peel paint."

The waitress looked slightly insulted, since this restaurant specialized in exotic coffees, then turned away without a word.

"I think you've hurt her feelings." Victoria let her gaze wander over his features, pleased at what she saw. The frustration and bitterness that had been reflected in his expression that first day were fading.

"Better her feelings than my taste buds. How can you stand to drink that stuff?"

"It's better than that turpentine you call coffee." They smiled at each other, finally accepting their sparring as a friendly exchange.

"What's the plan, boss?" She leaned forward, eager to get started, and even more eager to solve the burglaries. Her story would make the front page when it broke and Russ would finally have the satisfaction of jailing his tormentor.

"I picked up some radios. Nothing fancy, glorified kids' toys really, but they're the best I can do. I think they'll work for the short distances we'll be covering." He pulled out his napkin and began drawing the shape of the mall. ''Here's what we'll do.''

He outlined his thoughts in careful detail. Victoria didn't like the idea of staying in the car, but agreed she should be near the pay phone to call for the police when they were needed.

''Do you want me to make the call when we see the break-in, or wait?''

Russ hesitated, then looked up to study her, as if he were trying to gauge her depth of commitment to helping him do this on his own. ''Will you wait until I tell you to call?''

''Yes.'' She didn't want to do it. She didn't want him to take any risks, but felt he deserved the chance. She would watch carefully and if the least little thing went wrong, she'd call in spite of his instructions.

''I've got handcuffs and I plan to carry a gun—''

''Russ, you can't.''

''As a private citizen, I have a right to carry a gun as long as it isn't concealed and I'm not creating a disturbance. Since there won't be anyone around to be disturbed, except for our bad guys of course, there's no problem.''

She shifted uneasily. Guns made it more real, more dangerous. She didn't want anything to happen to Russ, not now. Not when she'd finally found someone she was willing to share her life with.

Lowering her lashes to conceal her feelings, she studied Russ. Did he feel the same way? He'd already indicated he wanted to stick around, to see her after the case was over. Could she convince him to make it permanent? Would she have the courage to bring up the subject of marriage to him if he failed to ask the question?

''We'll just watch and hope for the best. If the time line we worked out is right, tonight is when they'll hit.'' Russ paused to make some illegible marks on the napkin. ''I don't know how many there will be, but I suspect it has to be two or three in order for them to be in and out so fast. We have to be ready for anything, and the best way to do that is to play 'what if.' What's the worst possible thing that would happen and what could we do about it?''

Russ's coffee arrived and they each ordered a sandwich. Then he proceeded to present several sets of different circumstances that terrified Victoria as they tried to work through a plan of how to deal with each of them.

Russ finished the last of his sandwich and eyed her leftover meal with interest. Without a word, she pushed her plate toward him, quiet terror eating away at her own appetite.

''Do you know how to shoot a gun?''

Victoria stiffened. ''Yes. I did a story on it once and did extensive research.''

Russ shook his head and opened his mouth to comment, but she interrupted him. ''I can handle a revolver or a semiautomatic and I can hit what I'm shooting at.''

''Good. I'll leave a gun under the seat of the car, just in case. Just don't think you're going to play the part of hero, Vicky. Stop and plan before you grab that gun and come out of the car.''

He watched her carefully. ''We should both go home and get some rest. It could be a long night. I'll pick you up at nine o'clock, so be ready.'' Pulling out her chair, he took her hand when she stood. ''Wear dark clothes.''

She followed him outside, striving to maintain her composure with determination. Russ was all business, all cop, with an attitude that was scaring her silly. When she went into these things alone, there was little planning and less thought. It made it seem less dangerous, less real. And in the past, she'd had little to lose. Now she had everything to live for and she hardened herself to stay cool and do what needed to be done to protect that life.

*   *   *

"Victoria, can you hear me?" Russ shook the walkie-talkie in disgust. He should have known better than to put his faith in what was an overadvertised children's toy, but he'd had little choice. He needed to stay in contact with Victoria and he had no access to the powerful radios he'd used at the police department.

Another thought disturbed his aggravation and he almost gave up on the entire stakeout. Victoria could have very well chosen to ignore him and go her own merry way. It wouldn't have been the first time he'd seen her do it. And somehow, he doubted it would be the last.

They'd planned the evening very carefully and they each had their own assignments, Victoria's being the one that would expose her to the least amount of danger.

He hoped.

He prowled the outside of the building, silently cursing himself. This had been a stupid idea. It was almost an impossibility that he'd be able to pull it off by himself. A full stakeout team would have trouble with a building this size. It was just their luck that the next jewelry store on the list was in a sprawling mall.

But he had to try, had to have some sense of personal satisfaction when this was all over. He desperately needed to find a reason for all the pain, all the doubt, he'd been subjected to these past months.

Jayk would probably have Russ arrested or reprimanded for interfering with police business. The lieutenant couldn't have Russ suspended, since Russ technically didn't work for the department right now, but he could make Russ's life miserable.

Russ keyed the mike and called Victoria again. Only static answered him. He sighed and glared around the darkened parking lot. He'd have to go find her and make certain she was all right. If she was out skulking around in the bushes like he suspected, he'd handcuff her to the steering wheel of the car. That was the only way he would be confident enough of her location to be able to concentrate on his own job.

If he'd been with another police officer, he would have known what to expect. But Victoria was a free spirit who'd never managed to follow anyone's rules but her own.

Impatience reflected in every step, Russ started toward the front of the mall where he'd left her sitting in the car. From where she sat, she could view the entire west side of the building. That only left the back and the two sides for Russ to cover. Since the jewelry store was in the middle of the building, they'd decided the sides were a very remote possibility. That still left a lot of ground to cover.

A car door slammed in the distance as Russ rounded the first corner of the building. His footsteps sounded in the quiet of the night, reminding him of just how isolated the two of them really were. When the roar of an accelerating motor reached his ears, Russ tried to break into a limping run, his speed hampered by his injured leg. The pain increased until he finally had to give up and walk the remainder of the way.

A silent curse hovered on his lips until he finally reached the front of the mall. He turned into the front parking lot just in time to see a set of taillights wink in the darkness as a car rounded the corner and disappeared from sight.

Russ's vehicle sat a few feet away, dark and silent. And empty. He pounded his fist on the roof and muttered a few choice words before forcing his control back into place. Using his shirttail to cover his fingers, he eased open the front door and peered inside. The walkie-talkie was lying on the floor of the passenger side, a silent testimony to the failure of all his plans.

They hadn't covered this possibility in their game of ''what if.''

Russ leaned his forehead against the cool metal of the window frame and struggled for control. The silence echoed around him as he tried to force his brain into functioning like the well-trained machine it used to be. But always before, he'd been detached. Always before, the victim was just a nameless person.

This was Victoria, the woman he was slowly falling in love with.

Victoria had always insisted she could take care of herself and had proven that fact many times. The woman had the most amazing knack for getting into trouble, but her guardian angels must work overtime, because she also managed to slip back out of trouble again.

But this time, Russ had a profound feeling that she was in too deeply to get out by herself. This time, he'd have to find a way to help her.

And he didn't have a clue where to start.

Chapter Nine

The drive to Jayk and Kelly's home seemed to take forever. Russ knew he was wasting precious minutes by not stopping to call, but this was the type of news that was best delivered in person. And since he had no clue as to where to start looking for Victoria, a matter of fifteen minutes didn't seem too important.

He should have handcuffed her to the steering wheel. That had been his first inclination. If he had, then some sneak thief wouldn't have been able to spirit her off.

Of course, she also wouldn't have been able to make that all-important phone call, but he could have worked around that.

His mind turned over the little bit of information they'd managed to collect on the case so far. He worried each tidbit, dissected it, tried to put it together in different ways, but nothing worked. Victoria was gone and he hadn't the slightest idea who had taken her.

The porch light came on before Russ could pry himself from the car. Kelly was waiting with the screen door pushed open, a worried frown on her face. ''What brings you way out here at this hour?''

''I need to see Jayk. It's about the burglaries.'' He limped up the stairs, the pain in his leg worse than it had been in months. But then, he was demanding more of it than he had in a long time, too.

Kelly didn't need to ask which burglaries; she just silently ushered him inside, flicked on the coffeemaker, and waited until Russ had eased into a chair. Then she hurried off to find her husband.

When Jayk joined them, Russ outlined the events of the past few hours. Jayk's jaw tightened and he shook his head in disbelief, but he remained silent. It was Kelly who finally took out her frustration on Russ, something he felt he richly deserved.

''I can't believe you did this! How could you let Victoria put herself in that kind of danger?'' Kelly's already wild curls seemed to vibrate with her anger.

''You can't blame me any more than I already blame myself, Kelly. But just for the record, have you ever tried to stop Vicky from doing what she wanted?''

Kelly's anger deflated at his words and she managed a slight smile. ''Yes, and it's almost as impossible as stopping you. What a pair the two of you make.''

Jayk leaned forward and pulled the phone closer. ''Enough of that, both of you. We've got a bigger problem right now and that's finding Victoria before she gets hurt. As much as I want that woman out of my life, I didn't want it to be permanent.'' His hand rested on the receiver as he tried to form the questions that would give him something, anything, to work on. ''Nothing on the car?''

Russ shrugged. ''A dark, older model, probably four-door. From the shape of the taillights, I'd guess a Buick.''

''You've just described several thousand vehicles in this town.'' Jayk ran a hand over his face. ''But I guess it does narrow it down a bit. The initials still mean nothing?''

The frustration dug deep into Russ's ego as he shook his head. He'd thought he could handle it, had been certain he could pull off the impossible.

He hadn't and now Victoria was going to pay the price.

She was pushed roughly to the floor of the car and ordered to keep her head down. Victoria's first inclination was to scream a protest and jab her attacker in the eye. But she curbed the desire and made herself act subdued and scared.

The scared part wasn't too difficult. She'd never found herself directly involved in the crime before, never been a helpless victim before. Her view had always been from the sidelines. Except for that one time, and then Russ had been there to save her. This time, he wasn't going to be able to help her.

The car lurched back and forth as they hurried to some unknown destination. When they stopped abruptly, Victoria clutched her purse closer and waited, her heart pounding. She just needed a few seconds and she could give Russ his case on a silver platter. But she had to wait for just the right opportunity.

A tall, heavyset man grabbed her arm and dragged her from the car. She glared at him, but bit her lip to hold back her anger. The two men took her into a darkened warehouse and roughly shoved her into a corner. The cold concrete hurt her knees as she fell, but she huddled submissively.

"Watch her while I get the lights," one man ordered.

The second man stood there, just looking at her as Victoria glared back.

When the lights flooded the room, she blinked, trying to adjust to the sudden brightness. When the first man returned, she watched him carefully, hoping to note an unusual mannerism or something that would help her identify him even though he wore a ski mask.

"What are we going to do with her, Stan?"

"Shut up, you idiot. No names." Stan paced the floor, anger reflected in every step. "We've apparently been found out by someone. But not the police. Right, honey?"

Refusing to answer, Victoria tucked her legs under her, hoping her chance would come soon. Fear was threading its way through her and she needed to act before it took complete control.

"Doesn't matter." Stan turned away. "There's someone out there who'll want her back. There's money to be made on ransoms and it might be easier than jewelry stores."

"I don't like that. You do hard time for kidnapping. Let's just leave her here and go do the jewelry store. You said this was the last one anyway. Let's cut our losses and get out while we can.''

''Quit whining. We need to—''

A crash, followed by the yowling of a cat, sounded somewhere outside the warehouse. When both men spun around to look, Victoria took her chance. She grabbed the gun from her purse as she jumped to her feet. ''Freeze, gentleman.''

They both turned back to her, stunned at the sight she presented. Her feet were braced and she knew she was holding the gun like a professional would. That alone had to make an impression on the men. ''Let's take those masks off so I can see who I'm talking with. Then maybe one of you can find something for me to tie you up with.''

Both men pulled off their masks, and the unnamed man offered to get a ball of twine several feet away.

Stan punched his partner in the chest. ''Don't be so helpful. If we're not tied up we have a chance of taking her. There's two of us and one of her.'' He took a step toward her.

''Actually, there's seven of me and only two of you.'' She clutched the gun tighter, trying to mask the trembling of her hands.

''How do you figure that, lady?''

"I have six bullets as my backup. Care to argue with them?" She almost smiled as the man paled, then turned his back and let his partner tie his hands.

"Both of you, on your stomachs." When they were both lying down, Victoria tied the other one, then for good measure, tied their feet and looped the extra string through their hands. She double-checked her handiwork, then sat back to try to slow her racing heart. If this was an example of what cops did every day, she knew she didn't have the nerves for it.

When her breathing had slowed to a reasonable rate, she opened her purse and started digging. With a frustrated sigh, she turned back to the two men.

"I don't suppose one of you has a quarter I can use, do you?"

Jayk turned over the possibilities in his mind. "I guess I can put out an APB, increase patrols at the jewelry stores, and hope for the best. Our only other hope is that whoever has her plans to use her as a hostage and calls in with some sort of demand."

The phone rang as he reached for the receiver and with a quirk of his eyebrow he raised it and answered. Frowning, he pushed the button for the speakerphone and sat back.

"Lieutenant, I'm sorry to bother you tonight, but we've got some lady on the phone who insisted we call you. She said she'd only give the information to you because you're the only one who'd handle it right. Sounds like a real nut case to me. Do you want me to put her off?"

"What's her message?"

There was a moment's silence while the officer talked on another phone. "Her name is Victoria Stephens and she wants you to meet her at a warehouse on Banyon Street. She says everything is under control, but you're the only one who will understand what needs to be done."

A collective sigh filled the room as Jayk asked for more details.

"She won't tell me, sir. And she says we shouldn't send a patrol car, just you. Could it be a setup? Should I call out the SWAT team?"

Russ almost laughed, relief flowing through his veins like the bubbles from a bottle of champagne. Not even the SWAT team was prepared for Victoria. She'd apparently taken on the bad guys and won, either by dumb luck or sheer, unadulterated nerve. Either way, she was safe.

"I'll take care of the matter, Sergeant." Jayk

stood and motioned for Kelly to go get dressed. ''I'll call in when I find out what's going on.'' He disconnected the call and glared at Russ.

''What's she up to, Russ? Why am I the only one who can help her?''

Russ couldn't control the slight shifting of his body. He was embarrassed now by his need to make the arrest, to have a personal vengeance. Suddenly, all that mattered was that Victoria was safe, that he'd have a chance to hold her and tell her how he felt about her. ''I told her I needed to make the arrest, that I didn't want to be left out while the police handled it.''

''You realize if the captain gets wind of what I'm about to allow, he'll have my job and you'll probably end up in jail.''

''Yeah, just like old times, huh?'' Russ couldn't stop the grin that pulled at his mouth. It was going to be okay. Victoria was all right and if Russ's suspicions were right, she had his suspect tied up in a neat little package right now. In fact, she probably knew more about the case than the police ever would.

Jayk sighed. ''You and Kelly are my backup. I still trust you two more than anyone else on the force, so it should be no problem. Of course, when this hits the press, I'll have done it single-handedly. Is that okay?''

''You're the boss. I just want to look the guy in the face and ask him why he shot me.''

Kelly came downstairs, slipping a gun into her purse as she handed a holster and gun to her husband. ''I woke Jimmy and told him we'd be gone for a while. He'll take care of the kids. Shouldn't Russ have a weapon?''

Jayk shook his head. ''I must be crazy. Let him have the shotgun in the car. It'll give him that macho feeling.''

They all laughed as they hurried outside. Quiet plans were made on the drive into town, then they dispersed and entered the building from different entrances, not exactly certain what they'd find.

Jayk stepped inside, sticking to the shadows, and he almost laughed out loud at the scene presented to him. Two men lay on their stomachs, hands tied behind their backs, while Victoria stood guard over them with her gun clutched in both hands.

''Did you call for assistance, Victoria?''

She whirled around, then smiled when she saw him. ''These gentlemen thought they were going to hold me for ransom. But they forgot to take the gun out of my purse first. I guess that means I win and they lose.''

''Couldn't you have turned them over to a uniform? Why drag me from a warm bed?''

"Because you're the only one who would understand that Russ needs to be here, that he needs to help." She glanced into the shadows behind Jayk hopefully. "Do you know where he is?"

"I'm right here." Russ stepped out of the shadows and stopped directly in front of her. "Thank you for understanding, Victoria." The simple words didn't begin to cover what he was feeling, but they'd have to do for now. At least until he could get her alone and show her how grateful he was. "And if you ever pull a stunt like that again, I'll personally throttle you."

Unable to resist, he wrapped his fingers around the back of her neck and tugged her forward, pressing a hard kiss on her lips. "I love you, lady." And this time, he knew he truly meant the words.

Jayk sent Kelly to call for a patrol car while he advised the two suspects of their rights. While they were waiting for help to arrive, Jayk tried to find out the details of what happened to Victoria.

"They came out of nowhere and I didn't have a chance to do anything. They thought they just had another helpless female on their hands." She ignored Russ's disbelieving snort. "But I'd slipped the gun into my purse earlier, so I knew it was just a matter of finding the right moment, and I'd have the advantage.''

''I told you to leave it under the seat.''

''Well, it's a good thing I didn't listen, isn't it?''

Russ laughed, his relief making him almost giddy. ''When do you ever listen to a mere mortal like me?''

Victoria grinned her answer, then pulled out her notebook and began jotting down notes.

''Do I detect the sound of a little reporter's pen scratching?'' Jayk asked with a grin.

''Yeah, and I'm close enough to hear it, just like I promised you,'' Russ answered.

''Hey, I got my story and Russ got his arrest. Since everything came out just the way it was supposed to, we can all relax again, right?''

Jayk and Russ exchanged a wary glance over Victoria's head. Russ was beginning to suspect he'd never be able to relax again. Not with Victoria in his life in the capacity he wanted her to be.

Victoria glanced up. ''His car wasn't even close to the description I had. I'd have never found it; the colors were all wrong. I guess that's the last time I trust that informant.''

Jayk glared at her. ''How long have you had that description?''

She simply smiled at him and Russ resisted

the urge to kiss her again. "Oh, not very long. And since it was bad information, it doesn't matter, does it?"

"Are you sure you don't have a job offer in New York or something?" The sound of a patrol car outside drew Jayk's attention, but his eyes warned that they had more to talk about.

Kelly returned home while the others went to the police station to do the appropriate reports and interviews. Victoria gave her story to another officer, while Jayk directed the interviews of the two suspects.

When the formalities were completed, Russ paced the floor and drank the stale coffee, waiting, wondering. If Jayk got anything at all, he'd promised to share it with Russ on the side. The need to know gnawed at Russ, pushing aside everything else for the moment. There was plenty of time tomorrow to deal with Victoria, his career, and the rest of his life.

Victoria sat nearby and wrote furiously in her notebook. Suddenly, she stopped and walked over to Russ. Putting a hand on his arm, she halted his prowling, then put her arms around him and simply held on.

"I was so scared." Her voice carried a slight tremor.

Russ stroked his fingers over her hair. "Me too. I almost died when I found you gone."

She looked up, her blue eyes reflecting the shadows of her fear. "It's over now. You can get back to the business of healing so you can return to work. This department needs you, Russ."

He pressed her head against his shoulder, refusing to respond to her beliefs. Because he still didn't know if he'd ever be needed by anyone again. And the doubt was tearing him apart. He wanted to make plans, to propose marriage to Victoria and start a new life with her. But he couldn't. Not yet.

The door to the interrogation room snapped open and Jayk strode out, his lips set in a grim line. Victoria pulled away and waited beside Russ, her fingers curling into his in an offer of support.

"Do you remember Stanley Brown?"

Russ frowned, trying to match the name up with a case.

"You testified against him at a disciplinary action for the police department about four years ago."

The memory came flooding back and Russ almost groaned. "He'd been stealing from the businesses when he found open doors at night. I was the one who caught him in the act of loading a fax machine into the trunk of his patrol car.

''None of the businesses wanted to press charges, so the department settled for firing him. He said he'd get even, that I should watch my back because when I least expected it, he'd be there to get his revenge.''

''Yeah, that's the one.'' Jayk dragged his fingers through his hair.

''Why wasn't there a police report on it?'' Victoria asked.

''It was an internal investigation, so it's kept in a different set of files from the regular reports. That's why it didn't appear on Russ's list.''

''I didn't take him seriously.'' Russ stuffed his fists deep in his pockets, trying to resist the urge to punch something.

Jayk grimaced. ''We never take the threats seriously, Russ. But this one was for real. He hasn't been able to get work, lost his wife, his house, everything. Then he decided to use his knowledge of the alarm systems and the layout of the stores to his advantage. It was just pure coincidence when you caught him in the act. And he finally had his chance for retribution.'' Jayk paused thoughtfully. ''He wanted you to suffer the same way he had. He wanted you out of work permanently, but he didn't want you to die, because then you wouldn't have to endure what he had.''

''That's sick.'' Victoria leaned closer to Russ, the horror of the truth reflected in her eyes.

''Yes. And so is he, I suspect.'' Jayk turned away but Russ stopped him.

''The ring was his?''

''Yes. He'd lost it during the robbery, knew it was in that corner, but couldn't find it. He damaged the other cases in hopes of drawing any possible attention away from that location. I guess he didn't count on your determination.'' Jayk put his hand on Russ's shoulder, offering silent support. ''If we've got everything from you, go home, Russ. I'll call if anything new develops.''

''I want to talk to him, Jayk.''

Jayk shook his head.

''I deserve that chance. I need him to look me in the eye and tell me he tried to destroy me.''

''And then I'll have to take you to the floor when you take a swing at him. No way, Russ.''

Russ moved forward a step, testing Jayk's resolve, but Jayk held his place in front of his friend. ''I'm not going to let anything mess up this court case, Russ. I want this guy behind bars and letting you have a shot at him could be enough to get him off.'' Jayk gave Russ's shoulder a push. ''Let it go, bud. It's time for you to go home.''

Russ stood there, struggling with himself. He knew Jayk was right, he agreed with every word his former supervisor said, but the anger still burned deep inside, looking for a release. Finally, Russ forced his muscles to relax. He had no choice. The fight was over.

Victoria led him outside and he let her, still slightly dazed at the turn of events. An ex-police officer had been the one to take such nasty vengeance against him. And the man may have been much more effective than he'd ever realized. Not only had he stolen Russ's career, but Russ couldn't allow himself to commit to a future with a very special woman without the prospect of work.

''Are you okay?'' Victoria pulled his car door open for him and waited while he got inside.

''Yeah. I just need to let it all soak in. Do you need a ride home?''

She shook her head. ''I'm going to hang around a little longer, get some more information, then I need to go to the office and file the story while it's still fresh in my mind.'' She leaned inside and brushed her lips against his. ''I'll call you as soon as I can.''

The night passed in slow torment for Russ.

He finally got up at dawn and sat on his back patio, watching the sunrise. The sight had always given him hope before, sparking a need to move forward, to keep living. But suddenly it wasn't working anymore. The only thing that had kept him going these past months had been the need for vengeance, to see the case resolved and his attacker behind bars.

Now that it was over, what was left?

An image of Victoria flickered into his thoughts, and finally the hope began to burn. Once he was healed, he'd go back to work and convince her to share her life with him. Once again, life would be perfect.

The sunlight stabbed at his eyes and Russ slid on the mirrored sunglasses as he limped toward his car. The doctor's words still echoed in his mind. Russ had been given his final evaluation, hoping to hear he could get on with his career.

But the doctor had just eliminated that idea forever. The leg would never again be fully functional; there had been too much damage. And Russ knew the department would never accept him back as a street officer unless he was one-hundred-percent physically fit. His knee would barely make it if he were careful.

The stresses and strains of patrol work would destroy his leg.

His other option was a desk job but he knew that would drive him over the edge. To be so close to the action and never be a part of it would be worse torture than never working as a police officer again.

Yesterday, anything had seemed possible. Today, he knew nothing was possible. He couldn't ask Victoria to share his life if he had no job, no future. And he couldn't go back to the work he loved with a passion.

He dropped the doctor's evaluation off at the police department, simply leaving the form at the front desk so he wouldn't have to talk with anyone.

The drive home passed without registering and Russ soon found himself sitting in his favorite chair, once again feeling sorry for himself. The hours ticked past without notice as his numbed mind struggled to deal with the realities he'd been forced to accept today.

The front door opened, letting in a slip of the evening sun.

Russ didn't even look up. "Go away. I'm not buying anything."

"And I'm not selling anything, so quit growling at me."

Victoria's voice registered, but he refused to

look up and let her see the hopelessness in his eyes.

''News couldn't possibly travel that fast, so what are you doing here, Vicky?''

''Kelly called. She was worried about you.''

''I wish you women would quit interfering in my life.'' He just wanted to be left alone, to wallow in his misery. Maybe in two or three years, he'd make a stab at living again.

''You're pouting again.''

That brought his head up with a snap. Victoria was silhouetted in the doorway, a baseball bat braced on the floor. He should have laughed at the sight, but he couldn't.

''I'm not pouting.'' What had he ever done to deserve her in his life? What had he done to deserve falling in love with such a contrary woman?

''Where have I heard that before?'' She stepped closer and swept her hand around the room. ''Drawn shades, musty air, and you slumping in an old chair that's seen better days. If that's not pouting I don't know what is.''

He pushed the words through gritted teeth. ''I'm not pouting.''

She lifted the bat to her shoulder and came to stand beside him. ''I guess I'll just have to knock some sense into you then.''

His breath came out in a rush of exasperation. "Vicky, I'm useless. I can't work, can't take care of myself, can't support a family."

For once she didn't correct his use of her nickname. "Just because your leg is weak doesn't mean you can't do anything."

He held little hope of convincing her to leave, but maybe he could get her to give up on him. That thought brought a little twinge of rebellion, but he squashed it. He wanted to feel hopeless, because that was what his life was. "I can't do the work I was meant to do."

She knelt beside his chair, laying down the bat. "You can still marry me. We can still have a life together."

He watched her throat work as she gulped from nervousness. Giving into his need to touch her, he tucked a strand of hair away from her face. "I can't take care of you. And I won't be a kept man."

Her snort was very unladylike. "I have no intention of giving you a free ride either. Trust me, you'd earn your keep."

"How?"

"If I have to explain it, Russ, forget it. I thought I could still save you from yourself, but maybe that's not possible."

She stood and started to turn away but Russ grabbed her hand, desperate to keep her there, to torture himself with the impossible a little longer. He didn't want to be alone with his fears. He couldn't stand the silence of the house any longer.

"A man takes care of his wife, not the other way around."

She tucked her fists on her hips and glared at him. "Don't be so old-fashioned. There are other ways to do it."

"I can't be a good husband to you, Victoria."

"Then you'll just have to be the wife and I'll be the husband."

He frowned at her, trying to sort through her words, needing to understand what she was offering.

Shaking her head, she moved closer, resting her hand on his arm. "You can take care of the house, cook the meals, sort the socks, and raise the kids. I'll earn the living. I make a good wage; we can have a good life."

A spark of hope flared in his heart. "I don't think I'd have much luck getting pregnant."

She laughed, knowing deep inside that she'd convince him, that she'd have everything she'd ever wanted and not hurt anyone. "I'll still make the babies, but you can raise them. When I come home from work every night, I can't imagine a greater treat than having supper on the table, sweet-smelling kids eager to hug me, and a husband to rub my back.''

She watched some of the tension leave his face and knew she was winning. ''Maybe you could find something to do at home, some sort of home business, at least until your leg gets stronger.''

''I've always wanted to write a book.'' He offered the revelation almost shyly, as if he were waiting for her to ridicule him.

''Perfect. Police novels are hot stuff right now and you have all the experience to give them a flavor of reality.'' She sat in his lap, draping her legs over the arm of the chair and wrapping her arms around his neck. ''I've got a dictionary and the computer at my apartment, so we wouldn't even have to buy you any equipment.''

''Do you really think you could be happy with me?'' The doubts still lingered, but the hope was burning strong.

''I know I couldn't be happy without you. You've changed my life, Russ, and I never want to be all alone again. I want to share the insanity with someone and you're the one I choose. Marry me, Russ. Share the love, the laughter, the absolute wonder of life with me.''

His chuckle rumbled deep in his chest.

"Maybe you should be the fiction writer in the family. That was awfully pretty prose."

"I deal in facts, sir." She rubbed her nose against his before teasing him with a quick kiss. "And the fact is, I love you and I need you in my life. Will you marry me?"

When he said yes, all her doubts exploded, leaving her with a certainty that Madame Plotsky had been right. Victoria just had to have the courage to reach out and take what she wanted and the universe would work things out from there.

They'd been given a second chance at love, at life, at laughter. And Victoria had no intention of wasting one minute of it.

Epilogue

"I can't believe I'm really doing this." Jayk tugged at his necktie and squirmed like a little boy forced to sit on a hard church pew.

Kelly grinned at him tolerantly and straightened the necktie for the twentieth time that afternoon. "Just relax. It will all be over soon."

"No, it won't. It's just beginning. I wanted Victoria out of my life and now she'll be there forever. I can't believe Russ is really marrying her. I always knew he wanted revenge against me, but I didn't think he'd take it this far."

Kelly's surprise was almost comical. "Revenge? For what?"

"For hurting you, for not trusting you

enough to marry you when I should have. He's always held that against me.''

''You're paranoid, Taggert. Trust me, Russ has had more on his mind than just getting back at you.''

''I hope you're right. But either way, I'm stuck with that woman in my life forever.''

''You'll survive, tough guy. Trust me.''

Jayk groaned.

Victoria swept through the doorway, a vision in white lace.

Jayk forced a smile to his lips and held out his arm for her, ready to escort her down the aisle to her future husband, even if he did have more than his share of doubts and regrets.

Victoria hesitated, then turned terrified eyes toward Kelly. ''I can't do it. I can't go through with this.''

''It's just pre-wedding nerves, Victoria.'' Kelly went over and wrapped her arm around the bride's shoulders. ''You'll feel better when the ceremony is over.''

''When the ceremony is over it will be too late. I've made a mistake.'' Victoria picked up her skirt and turned to leave, but Jayk stopped her.

''You can't convince me that the Victoria Stephens I know would ever run from anything. That woman would stand up to anyone who got in her way in order to pursue what she believed in.'' He took her hand and pulled it through the crook of his elbow. ''You do believe in Russ, don't you?''

''Russ is too good for me. I'll make his life miserable.''

''Well, you've been swearing revenge on the entire police department for years. You won't have a better chance than this. With Russ to get you access to the inner sanctum, you can make all our lives twice as miserable.'' He started walking forward, dragging her with him.

Victoria resisted, then hesitantly followed him. Jayk leaned closer and whispered his next words. ''Besides, I know you love him and that alone is enough to overcome anything.''

She walked beside him silently as the music swelled around them. When he glanced over to see the effect of his words he saw a single tear trace a path down her cheek.

''Thank you, Jayk.'' Her words were barely a whisper, but Jayk smiled as he handed her over to Russ, knowing he'd just sealed his own fate. There wouldn't be another chance to get Victoria out of his life so he might as well learn to accept her. And maybe in time, he could even learn to like her.

The bride and groom smiled at each other,

then Russ leaned forward to lift Victoria's veil and kiss her before the ceremony could be started.

The minister cleared his throat three times before the couple broke apart. Then, he hurried through the vows, casting suspicious glances at the pair to make certain they were paying attention to what was being said.

When it was finally time for the official kiss, Russ swept Victoria into his arms and held her much longer than was proper while he kissed his new wife thoroughly.

He'd been given a second chance, with his career and his heart. He'd been allowed to try one more time.

And he'd come out the winner in every way.